4 -

THE SPORTING CLUB

THE
SPORTING
CLUB

Thomas McGuane

Farrar, Straus and Giroux • *New York*

for my brother John

Whirl is king.

—ARISTOPHANES

1

NORTHERN GENTLEMEN

Blucher's *Annals of the North* (Grand Rapids, Michigan, 1919) which perforce omits the human element and which minces the few words at its disposal, has this to say:

Centennial Club (formerly the Shiawasee Rod and Gun Club): Grandest of the original sporting clubs of the Northern Lower Peninsula, founded by the barons of lumbering who logged off the white pine stands of the Saginaw Country. Its charter was written in 1868 while the big timber was being converted to pioneer houses on the treeless prairies of the West. The operations of the Centennial Club are shrouded in well-guarded mystery. Nothing is known of its procedures but that membership is handed from fathers to eldest sons. The vastness of the Centennial land holdings is widely known: they extend from the Pere Marquette to the Manistee. A mounting body of evidence has pointed to the club's large influence in state and local politics. The grounds include many buildings of interest, principally the MAIN LODGE★★★★★ which is a distinguished early example of G. K. Truax's "country style" though much modified both by the capricious architectural tastes of early-time lumber barons and by the use of amateur Indian labor. Nearby are some smaller club buildings worth the visitor's attention. These include the GAZEBO★★★★ and a well-constructed TOOL–SHED.★ Tours are occasionally arranged during winter months.

Blucher is a little misleading (there has never been a tour); and like so many clubs, the Centennial Club has suppressed an accessible luxury in favor of roughing it. Anyone looking for splendor would find it plain. Even the tool-shed disappoints.

This morning, two men rode along the sandy miles between the front gate and the upland slope upon which the club had located its buildings. Jack Olson, the manager of the club, drove the jeep with certitude over the disrepair of the road. James Quinn sat beside him and studied the woods. Behind the two, just unloaded from the club's twin-engined Beechcraft, loomed Quinn's gear. Quinn was here to rest and that always seemed to require a lot of equipment; though if Vernor Stanton was here no amount of it would save him. A sharpshin hawk wheeled low into the blue strip of sky over the road, its long legs trailing a brown curve of mouse, flew ahead of them for a moment and swung into the woods again. Quinn was beginning to see how he could be chiseled out of his recuperation and he was afraid to ask about Stanton. He knew he would have to ask; but it was a minute before he could go through with it.

"All right," Quinn said, "tell me."

"He's here."

"Is he."

They drove on. Quinn stared at the double gearshifts of the transmission and transfer box.

"He has his wife with him, you know," Olson said.

"So you think that will help."

"Well, so much of the old trouble started—"

"Yes—" Quinn encouraged.

"With women, right?"

"That's your boy. *Whew*. That's what I was thinking."

"And if he could just—" Olson began anew, encouraged.

"Say it, Jack. If he could just—?"

"Get his ashes hauled about sixty times a day—"

"Easy now. You think that would quiet him? Well, I do too. That would quiet most anything, wouldn't it? After all?"

"I guess." Olson was lost in thought.

"I mean just what kind of a girl is this?"

"Oh, no. Just a girl. But I mean, something, right? Wouldn't you think? Nobody sees him. He's been very quiet." Quinn agreed. He gazed out upon the familiar savannahs and stands of pine slashing. Then they turned onto a narrower road so frequently marked with rainpools that Olson engaged the four-wheel drive. Now cedars were around them and the road was very slightly flooded so that when they hit clay and the rear end swam a little, Olson accelerated to bring it back in line. The ferns made their false floor in the woods and every shaft of sun was whirling with insects. They climbed again slowly.

"One other thing though. He built this dueling gallery

in his basement." Quinn looked at Olson. They were coming now along the last climb to the plateau.

"For what?" he asked. Olson turned his thin, intelligent face against the light and looked away from Quinn as though this were the first time he was giving it real consideration. The jeep bucked under them lightly.

"Eventualities," Olson said as if picking up the word in his hand. Quinn recognized Stanton in this. God help us, he thought. They stopped in front of the main lodge.

"I'll go see for myself." Behind the lodge was the forest. In front of it was a wide, manicured green compound encircled by a cliff of heavy pine. The main lodge was an immense three-story building with a bleached and shallow blue-gray mansard roof. In the middle of the compound was an octagonal screened gazebo called the Bug House, and beside it a tall metal flagpole with its slack ropes hitting musically. Quinn made arrangements for his place to be aired and swept and for his mail to be brought down. Then he headed down the dry, beaten trail that led out of the compound to Stanton's place. In a minute, he stopped for a nervous easing of his bladder, then went on where trees crowded, tall sunless pines blown out of the ground like jets of dark gas. Stanton's house was virtually without a yard. Quinn walked out of the woods three feet and was against the first step of the porch. He had gotten just this far when Stanton stepped, or rather thrust, out onto the top step. His muscular frame was covered only by the pleated linen shorts he wore and sweat ran down his chest. In his right hand hung a dueling pistol. "The true

Quinn," he said in his heroic manner; "this is an ugly surprise." Quinn ascended the steps.

"I've come to meet your new wife since you never troubled me with a wedding invitation."

"Well, come on in and introduce yourself to her." He turned back into the darkness. "Dat's what I do all de day long.—Janey!" he called. "Janey!" He led Quinn down the hall. "Off on one of her peerless nature jaunts." Quinn plunged his hands in his pockets and followed the barefoot and sweating Stanton. "Head of moose," Stanton said with a rotary movement of his left hand as he passed the trophy. They crossed the big, timbered living room. "Doorway to improved cellar."

Quinn followed Stanton down headlong steps to a lighted cellar. Odors of fresh paint, fiber insulation and dampness combined strangely. The first room was a bar and library with books, many of them good editions, swollen with moisture and neglected. Stanton made drinks and led Quinn into the next room, the dueling gallery. This was a serious place, painted like a ship's boiler room and lit like a surgical theater with a long row of egg-crate nonglare lights. They filled the room with a delicate electrical hum. At either end of the room were human silhouettes. Each had a red circle around the heart that enclosed the numeral ten. The other regions of the body were similarly defined with black perimeters that enclosed smaller numbers. Quinn considered it a stroke of surprising romanticism to award the heart ten points. A modern target would indicate a grand slam for the straight shot, from behind, to the skull, or perhaps a combination parlay for a disabler to the spine and finishing shot through the roof of the mouth. These targets had faces which were serene and Mediterranean and their eyes followed you around the room waiting to be shot.

"Admit I've improved the cellar," said Stanton, and Quinn felt he was stalling. Next to the entrance was a cabinet and he pulled open its door. "Come look here." Inside, on small felt-covered hooks, a dozen pairs of dueling pistols hung upside down by their trigger guards. Stanton took down a pair and handed one to Quinn. "French and without price. Made by Jean Baptiste Laroche, Paris, middle eighteenth century. They came with jasper flints which were purely decorative and had to be replaced. There is a fitted case for the convenience of the seconds who carry the instruments to the scene of the crime as if it were no more than a Dopp kit; a powder flask of the thinnest possible gold, instruments for cleaning and a mold that casts six perfect bullets at a throw."

The gun Quinn held was slender and heavy. The stock was oiled, dark walnut, the barrel long and octagonal. A pair of small, silver-chased dragons held the lock in place; and their flaming tongues curled around the hammer.

"Come on," Stanton said, "provoke me. We'll have a duel."

"All right. I disapprove of the stupid waste of money."

"That will do nicely." He took out a work glove from his sweaty hind pocket and flipped Quinn in the face with it. "I tell you, Pablo, I am provoked. Let's load the guns. *Vamonos!*" He took Quinn's weapon and charged it, seating the patched bullet with a small ramrod that slipped down the barrel making a half turn with the rifling. He loaded the second pistol in the same way, then primed the two guns with finer powder and held them out to Quinn next to each other, the knurled, acorn butts pointed in opposite directions. Quinn took one with amusement and cocked it with the solid complicated click of more than one thing falling into place, took a few steps and set his heels on the single line that divided the gallery in two. "One of us will have to count the paces."

"I will," Quinn said. "Otherwise we'll get foul play."

Stanton lined up behind him, heel to heel, and Quinn could feel Stanton's back radiate moistly through his shirt. They were alike in height though Stanton was much more heavily built. He was left-handed and the two pistols clicked together once.

"Ready?"

"I'm ready," said Stanton.

Quinn counted. At ten he turned on his heel and raised the dueling pistol. He looked down the clean plane of its barrel, saw Stanton's head quaver upon the blade of its front sight and bleed away in the slight glare of light. He began to feel the weight of the gun in his upper arm. He saw Stanton standing sideways, one hand on his hip, tilting slightly back from the waist, the head tilted back too and the narrowed eyes; Quinn thought that this was what a real duelist must look like. Then there was the flash and report of Stanton's pistol. Quinn went down feeling the pain open like a talon in his chest. He was on his back. He held himself upright on his elbows as Stanton ran whooping toward him, the row of electric bulbs streaming out of his head behind him. When he got to Quinn, Quinn raised his own gun with a seizure of hatred and fired. Stanton disappeared in the flash, bellowing, "Good God!" He snatched away Quinn's pistol. "Get off your backside, you candy ass! Wax bullets! Order of the day for dueling practice! Strictly order of the day!" Stanton was disgusted and Quinn looked at him, feeling the slow draining of hatred from his brain. He got to his feet gritting his teeth from side to side and peeled up his shirt. Over his heart was a circular welt, red at the edges and very white at the center, like a great wasp sting. He still felt frightened and, now that it was over, unnaturally light. This was a time when he would have liked to have shown himself quite solidly but he knew his eyes still moved with excessive speed and his hands trembled: Stanton never missed such things.

"Everyone told me you were slipping, Quinn, and I'm beginning to believe it."

"I'm not slipping," Quinn breathed. Stanton began to calm down. Quinn tucked in his shirt. "You scared me shitless."

"I see that I did. You look chastened. The fire is out in your great bunny's eyes. Well, you'll have a chance to recoup your emotional losses. This is a great spiritual exercise."

"Where did you ever get the idea?" Quinn asked blandly.

Stanton took the question seriously: "Where? Puerto

Rico. A professional twenty-one dealer had just paraded around me with a revolver and I lost such a terrific amount of face in front of a girl I was in love with that I considered defenestration. In my emotional exhaustion I decided that the only thing which could save me would be to always be prepared for the duel."

"How did I figure into this?"

"I thought if I blasted you once good I would get a couple more challenges out of you. Practice is not at all the same on a paper target."

Quinn wanted to go. They went up and into the living room again. "Head of moose," said Stanton; then, indicating the stairway asked, "See my sign?" Quinn looked; a metal placard read POST NO COITUS. He recognized this as another of Stanton's tests and waited patiently for the question. It came right away: "What do you think of it?" Quinn had a violent feeling of not requiring Stanton's tests, but he was alert enough to think: Probably it begins here. He answered that he thought it was in bad taste and was not at all moved when Stanton told him he would have laughed at it before.

He went through the woods to his own place, fingering the raised circle through his shirt, gently because it was quick to hurt. Son of a bitch, he thought; after all this time, this was more of the same; it had begun long ago with a punch in the face from Stanton that removed a tooth and lacerated his tongue badly enough that the tooth, presumed lost, floated out a day later from the cut—all because Quinn had said, purely on speculation, that there was no God. Nevertheless, Quinn had been caught napping again; and that is why, afterward, Stanton thought he looked chastened. He was.

He came into view of his house and it revealed anew its unwarranted glory. The house had been built by his great-grandfather and his grand-uncles and though it was well made, it had required considerable repair and attention since before the Second World War. Doing things in a hurry was by now a tradition in Quinn's family and there was some suspicion that green wood had been used in its construction. It was full of otherwise unexplainable gaps in its joining and invited the weather if it wasn't constantly attended. Still, Quinn was unable to imagine any kind of gradual decline of the house. Because he was so sure that it stayed together by some subtle, frangible system, he imagined that it would go all at once—collapse, the roof coming in like an enormity, blasting sunlight and dust from every opening and crevice.

Inside, the house was clear, sunny, its seven rooms swept and polished. A current International Harvester calendar hung on the wall of the living room; underneath were fifteen more, the latest showing a male model in tool-jeans mounting a combine. The crystal cabinet still held his arrowhead collection. The rooms were all underfurnished as is usual with summer places. The spare and unupholstered furniture suggested the house's long use as an operational center. Whatever sentiment it held could as easily have collected around the polished bars of a jungle gym or the packed sand of a bear garden.

Anyway, it pleased him to see it and he went into his old bedroom and lay down.

The minute his face touched the nubbed cotton chenille spread and he tried to doze off, his mind began to operate at full speed, thrusting him, against his will, back into his office on a recent day, a Monday, when his secretary, Mary Beth Duncan, was to have been on vacation and he had looked forward to a day in the empty office, undoing her more odious mistakes, refusing to answer the phone, smoking and talking graciously into the dictaphone, drafting letters of supply and demand, request and compliance—shapely paragraphs of clean business prose. But Mary Beth had given up a day of her vacation to take care of back work. Quinn was more than bitter at seeing her and tried to go quietly into his own office. "You don't see me, Mr. Quinn!" she sang as he entered, "I'm on vacation!"

"Right you are, Mary Beth. And get this: if you bring me the recent paperwork on American Motors, I won't pay any attention to you at all."

Mary Beth closed her eyes and shook her head. When he was finished, she cried, "You don't see me! I'm on vacation! You can't even see me!"

"Only this small—"

"You don't see me! I'm on vacation! You don't see me!" Quinn flung shut his office door, spilling papers, aghast. Mary Beth's sourceless cries continued to come through the door and lodge in his head. He sat down in his chair in an attempt to restrain himself. If she hadn't come, he could have spent the day like the businessman-savant he knew he could be; it was worse than that, too, the voice of that ass outside more like a steam whistle than anything human. He knew he should have fired her long ago. But he couldn't do it. He couldn't have fired Lizzie Borden from the same position. He saw things from too close up. He would have liked above all things to pare this trait away. A businessman who saw employees as people was finished. Meanwhile, Mary Beth's voice died away to, "All right, Mr. Quinn, all right for you! See if I care." Quinn calmed down. He asked himself how the day might be resurrected without his resorting to medication. He called Mary Beth on the interoffice phone. He told her that this was a place of business and that he wasn't going to have another of her Halloweens. Therefore, get to work or get out. The inevitable enraged weeping began an instant later, directed, he knew, at the resonant heart of his door. He yelled, "I have my life to live, too, you know! Do you know that?" He got no answer.

There was work to do. He was close enough to his success to be spurred on by amazement. The stacks and inquiries that piled up every day were food for the company that had acquired an almost animal life in his mind. The factory was an organism that must be fed by the sales department; the expensive and periodical retooling that kept the factory up to date was a necessary medical expense. The thought, even in mockery, would have struck him as absurd a year before. He would not have been able to imagine the sensitivity with which this great animal could respond to his ministrations. The company had seemed beyond human control and he had not been interested. Now the four connected Quonset buildings that held the heavy machinery, punch presses and forklifts seemed delicate enough to be tuned like musical instruments. There were rules of supply and storage that had visible effect; man hours, overhead and production soon became palpable facts.

A month after he took over the company, it was on the edge of bankruptcy. This fact alone brought him to life. Four hundred and fifty men were faced with the loss of their jobs. It was their pitiable luck, Quinn thought, to find themselves with a bored only child dabbling at the controls in ennui. But conscience had unlocked his energy. In Detroit, where the contemplative philosophies had made few inroads, the loss of so many livelihoods could still be seen as serious. At the same time—though his own more or less *rentier* position made his problems look theoretical—the thought alone that he could have wrecked a fifty-eight-year-old business in one month flat gave him an acute sense of his own powers. He began to abandon his nostalgia for the life of freedom, began to admit how really bored he had been at it, and he began to take an interest. Within a short time he found himself working like one possessed.

A light rain made the pine barrens bleary and the river dull. It fell for two solid days. Quinn stayed indoors and read thick wet periodicals. Most of them were his mother's fashion magazines, with page after page of epicene models writhing on lava flows in mortal constipation, or gazing at a crazy and unfriendly sun as if this were it unless we find water. He didn't see anybody for a while and looked up from time to time at the rain rippling over the windows.

When the weather broke and cleared, he came out squinting. Snails had crawled halfway up the door and were stuck in the sunshine, horns retracted, tracks dry as varnish. Quinn flicked them away and went back inside to dress for fishing. He dressed warmly because the river was still full of snow melt. He carried his waders over his shoulder and went down the hill in back that was so steep you had to grab poplar saplings to keep your footing. At the bottom was a plank walk that crossed the marshy ground behind the river. After that, he saw the Pere Marquette clear and fast and very slightly coffee-colored between its banks. Straight in front, he could see the details of the bottom behind the imperceptible surface. Downstream, it mirrored sky and trees, curled like molten silver at a fallen spruce and made a pool. Opposite Quinn was a high, steep bank, bare of large trees, called Harrison's Rollway, where lumbermen had rolled skinned logs into the river. He could see a half dozen good trout rising now in the pool and began to move toward it. The air was full of mayflies, females with yellow egg sacs that Quinn knew could be imitated with the Lady Beaverkill. They touched his face lightly and their wings flickered in the peculiar light as he worked to string the heavy, bellied line through the rod's guides and attach the long platyl leader. Now the rises were breaking out in the slicks behind the boulders and in the small tongues of current that ran between them. He put on the waders and carried the rod butt first through the woods to get below the pool. The cold bog smell of spring came very strong the minute before he stepped into the river. He crossed a few yards to get a casting angle and felt the cool, round pressure of river on his legs. By the time he was in position, eight fish were feeding steadily in a line, facing upstream as always.

He made his false casts carefully, the lengthening line up high on the sunlight and the rod beginning to flex its full length into his hand. With his left hand holding the free line below the reel, he adjusted the tension of the cast so that the bow of line was correct and satisfactory. He finished the cast. The line straightened before him. The fly floated down and touched the water. It glided, then vanished. The line went tight when he lifted the rod. The rod was now bowed toward the straight line that swung out of the pool to the main stream in the middle where it was furrowed and marked with the silver arrows of the suntrack. Quinn held the rod high. He felt the curve of it lose rigidity. The fish broke and so began to lose ground. When it broke again it was splashy and without violence and came slowly to the net. At the net, it bolted once more and swung around behind but a moment later was in hand, a trout of two pounds that Quinn, with his thumb securely under the gill covers, held first against the trees and then against the sky before he put it in his creel. He rinsed the crushed fly in the water to rid it of slime which would sink it, blew hard on it until its hackles were upright and the false wings of feather stood out from the hook. He began his casting once again. He shortened the timing of his first cast so that the line cracked very slightly like a whip and there was a small cloud of vapor in the air where the fly had been. The fly was now absolutely dry and when it landed on the water it stood high on its sharp hackles and floated the way an insect does.

When the mayfly hatch was finished and the fish had quit feeding, he had five good trout. On the way back to his cottage, he paused four times to open the wicker creel and look in at the trout he had put in wet ferns and arranged in a hierarchy of magnitude.

Quinn saw the back of Stanton's head bent to the open creel. "You can't do this. I want all details." He straightened up and Quinn glimpsed the fish bright and spotted in the ferns. He closed the wicker lid.

"I have no secrets," he said simply.

"You're just better than I am?"

"Now you're talking," Quinn said. He saw the truculence coming on, blunting Stanton's features.

"You've had to deal with me once," Stanton said hopefully.

"Yes, yes, I remember. Would again too."

"You would—?"

"Oh, sure." Quinn was eager to get his own back. The welt on his chest, now the color of plum, reminded him. But when they were in the dueling gallery, his nerves came back with the sudden memory of his last experience. He didn't want to be hit again. On the other hand, he wanted to stick Stanton if he possibly could. Then Stanton's wife came down the stairs, three at a time and, out of breath, introduced herself as Janey. "How do you do?" said Quinn, pleased with her. She wasn't what he expected. He expected something off Palm Beach with a lot of jaw, Jax slacks and attitudes. Instead, this girl had a fine, open-eyed ingenuousness that would have been poison to the kind of arm-pumping good sport Quinn had expected. Her mouth, by an almost invisible margin, did not close and its shape was clarified by the dark line. Her cheekbones were distinct, either broad or high, he wasn't sure; his study was making her jumpy. Quinn could have followed her around admiring her for a long time before actually wanting to lay hands on her.

Stanton took down a new set of pistols. These were percussion guns of the nineteenth century, made in Charleston, South Carolina, and had not been fired before. Janey said it was too bad to shoot them after so many years; couldn't they sword fight? Stanton looked over at her and went on loading the pistols. When he was finished, he presented Quinn with his choice. Janey counted this time, in Old Church Slavonic she called it, though Quinn suspected. Stanton said she could count to ten in nineteen major languages including Tel Aviv. It threw Quinn off. He at first thought it was funny in a nervous-making way. But by the time they got toward ten, he was fingering the trigger nervously, not knowing what number they were on and having to turn when the counting stopped to find Stanton already facing him. He fired a bad shot and at the same time received an indescribably painful hit in the center of his upper lip. Tears sprang to his eyes. Stanton smiled with the placidity of an *Annunciation*. Quinn handed him the discharged pistol with its sulphurous odor and hammer closed tight on the uselessly spent percussion cap, and went out of the house without a word.

By nightfall, the Stantons had lured him back for dinner. He swiftly drank too much and then finished half a pot of coffee to clear his head. His lip was swollen in a uniform protuberance so much like an auto bumper that Stanton giggled and held the sides of his seat.

"What about another chance?" Quinn said hotly.

"It wouldn't be fair."

"Let me judge."

"Not a chance. I've come to think of you as a sitting duck." Stanton's mouth was poised, ready to start into laughter. Next to him the bride dusted her strawberries with sugar from a small silver spoon.

So Stanton had this minute victory of refusal. But Quinn felt that he had stymied him on the larger issue simply by refusing to play, to fall into the old habit of scheming against the other members of the club, to see what was funny about the sign hanging over the stairway. Quinn felt that for once he held a subtle advantage. Stanton spoke. "How is your business, may I be so bold to ask?" Was this a lead shot or just a question?

"It's all right," Quinn said, cards very close now, almost not sporting.

"You realize that I don't work."

"Yes, I do."

Janey said, "It's like having a child in the house." Her voice was low and sweet. "He swarms." She had some kind of accent.

"You do just fine with me, sugar."

"I know I do, Vernor," she explained. He wasn't listening to her. "But you do seem to . . . *swarm*."

"Okay, Janey, time to hang up the jock," Stanton said to Quinn.

"Vernor fails to work, you see."

"Hang it up, Janey. Hang up the old jock." Stanton was patient and instructive. Then he turned completely to Quinn in order to exaggerate what he pretended to ignore. "Well! You've done right smart since you took over that firetrap factory of yours, have you not?"

"I've done well."

Janey flattered Quinn by looking at him with interest. She was so balanced and her gazing, slate eyes so serene that she made Stanton next to her look as overgrown as a Swiss Guard or an Alaskan vegetable; but, in fairness, he hadn't found his brilliant and destructive pitch yet and Quinn himself was rancorous for having been shot in the lip. So the game had stalemated prematurely.

"But still the solution seemed to you to direct your attention to Papa's company store." This was unfair of Stanton; it had become impossible without any kind of refereeing. Quinn spoke slowly.

"The company store makes an excellent punching bag for my frustrations and it appears that I am to be frustrated. Every time I slug it, it gets more profitable."

"What amazes me is your bravery, walking in cold." Stanton was trying to make it up; but with Janey watching, Quinn liked this bit of characterization.

"I learned. I made a lot of mistakes."

"Seems you learned all too well," said Stanton. "You're caught." Smug, he sipped his brandy conclusively.

"I know I am. I want to be." Quinn couldn't beat him at wit; but he thought he had a chance on the honesty count.

"Is it very dull?" Janey asked.

"Hang it up," said Stanton, deliberately misinterpreting. "You needle my friends and I'll kick your ass." She turned to him and Quinn studied her. She wasn't there any more. Very discreetly, she had departed. But hadn't Stanton been joking?

"Vernor's inactivity makes his mind run wild," she said from afar.

"Hang the sonofabitch up," said Stanton, dropping ringed, ominous hands to the table. Quinn knew that she couldn't be very safe around him. And because of that her remote backtalk had gallantry.

Saturday morning. Quinn walked to the main lodge for his breakfast. The midweek quiet was gone. Cars were parked under dusty pines and overdressed children in dresses and Eton suits circled the compound and ran in and out of the Bug House. The sun was high and lifted a square of hot light from the roof of the shed. The cars, too, even under their trees, were soaked with heat. Quinn walked through the kitchen entrance to the coolness of the dining rooms. He sat down at one of the linen-covered tables and surveyed. There was still the unnecessary number of china cabinets along the far wall. Overhead, the painted pressed-tin ceiling of nymphs and satyrs had the same prettiness and the same humorous light fixture bursting from one tin satyr groin. The walls were circled with pictures of early days, logging operations and sporting feats. Surmounting these were the stuffed trout and the stuffed heads of deer and bear; the multiplicity of unfocused glass eyes did as much as anything else to establish the mortuary atmosphere. On either side of the kitchen were two punt guns, poachers' weapons that could bring down a flight of ducks with a shot. These were fired on the Fourth of July. The wall whose window overlooked the Pere Marquette river was bare and on it were printed two clear pentagrams of sunlight. The room smelled of cedar shavings like a schoolhouse and the distant sounds of children made the quiet emphatic.

He read his mail as he ate and came across a letter that caused him to let a forkful of egg cool in midair: Mary Beth had taken it upon herself to supply price quotations for a small die-cast part that the company made; the price she quoted for the finished part was somewhat less than half the manufacturing cost, and the company was therefore swamped with orders. Quinn managed to finish his breakfast anyway before calling the office and telling Mary Beth what his feelings were, generally, about what she had done. He left her on the phone laughing and crying and telling him, "I hate you I hate you I hate you." Why me? Quinn inquired of himself.

He stopped outside at the edge of the compound. There was now a flag on the tall flagpole, standing out from its distant top like a new postage stamp. Behind the screens of the Bug House the small bandstand was visible with its chairs, its piano, its music stands and its shadowy, disused jukebox. The grass all around was brown in the exposure. From behind the main lodge came the same children's voices, the sound of chopping, and then heavy hands seized his ears. A falsetto cry came from behind: "Mumma! Mumma!" It was Stanton. He made Quinn guess over and over what day it was. Quinn couldn't do it. It was the day the Mackinac Bridge was to be dedicated.

"I don't want to go," said Quinn.

"I have my boat there."

"I don't want to go and I won't go."

"You're going."

"What'll we do? No, really, I don't want to go."

"This is an important day in our state's history you god damned loser and you're going to go."

"You and Janey go. Take pictures so that we can all pore over them ardently at some unspecified later date."

"If you don't go I'll spend considerable time and money to make your life a living hell."

"I'm telling you, Vernor. It isn't going to be the same this year. There is going to be no clowning."

Stanton looked at him. "I don't believe you," he said, looking.

The view of the water from the Mackinac dock was blocked at intervals by the tall steamers, all cleanly painted in gun-metal gray and white; and the glass panes of the great cabins and staterooms picked up the light of the very cold blue straits beyond. They walked the length of the dock, and the tall pilings next to them that were faced with strips of fire hose heaved and took up the slow shock of the steamers' movement. The private boats were moored beyond the steamers. The three of them stopped before a tall Matthews yacht that was heavily equipped with Rybovitch blue-water fishing modifications: outriggers, a tuna tower, gin pole and harpoon stand. The boat was covered with a fitted duck tarpaulin drawn tight as a trampoline at its grommets. The tarp stretched between the transom and the flying bridge; the radio direction finder was covered by a small fly of canvas that matched the tarpaulin. It was Stanton's boat and the name was on the transom in brass: *Lusitania*. Underneath that, the home port: Ponce, Puerto Rico. Quinn was thinking of the last time he had seen Stanton, helplessly and pathetically out of his mind in front of the Detroit Athletic Club. Afterwards, Stanton had headed south and this was how he'd gone.

They left the dock, passed a row of green highway department trucks and walked until they were at the thronged middle of Mackinac City with its weathered concrete and false territorial buildings. Stanton led and Quinn followed Janey through streets full of people who had come for the bridge dedication. The bridge itself was cordoned off by the state police. The three were balked; then Stanton led a retreat without explanation, downtown again to a dry-cleaning establishment. When he came out, he had three paper tags that he pinned to their chests; the tags read PRESS ONLY. They looked at each others' tags unconvinced.

Squinting past the great concrete fan of the entrance and past the toll gates, Quinn could see the bridge climbing, its towers and cables strewn against the sky, holding the vast and absurd booby trap together. Where the approach was closed off, black limousines with tinted windows began the ascent to the bridge's crown, and from behind those windows the myriad muted faces of nabobs gazed at the riffraff. These limousines were followed by a small parade of open convertibles, each with a queen seated on the furled top. There was a peach queen, a gasket queen, a celery queen, a lumber queen and finally, a slender, dark girl passed waving to the crowd, the smoked pickerel queen. A number of people tried to follow the queens onto the bridge. They were stopped by the police and howled in near-demented rage. Quinn, Stanton and Janey moved on to the entrance as though to walk straight through. A trooper stepped sideways into their path and Stanton said, "*Detroit Free Press,* officer. Will you get the hell out of our way, officer?" They walked through the unoccupied toll gates and onto the bridge where the concrete apron fell away to open grating through which the water of the straits was visible.

The bridge rose away in front of them, up between the two great towers that slung cables thicker than trees; and under his feet Quinn saw the dark water ticked with whitecaps fade to solid blue as they climbed. At first he saw nothing ahead except the smooth, ascending grate surface of the bridge. But after a short time, the dedication party was visible, its flags, buses, limousines and platforms gathered between towers like a distant hill town. Someone was talking over a loudspeaker, the voice indistinct on the wind. A lake freighter passing under the bridge, tremendously diminished beneath them, poured smoke from its oval stack that you could smell as it came up through the grating. As they went, not talking, figures began to resolve themselves out of the cluster between the towers. They approached and saw the dedication party, a crowd of perhaps a hundred. On the platform a man was making a speech in Canadian French into a wall of smiling, upright, uncomprehending Michigan burghers who smiled at him while they talked to each other. The speaker's hair was tossing and the sheaf of papers he held rustled uncontrollably in his hand. When his speech began to stumble, he looked down at this sheaf and his eyes widened with real ferocity.

Stanton beckoned. He was standing next to a bus designated STATE LEGISLATURE over its windshield. It was surrounded by parked limousines. Beyond the bus there was nothing but sky and lake. They followed Stanton as he pushed the folding door and climbed in. It was quiet and pleasant inside. They were out of the wind and no longer had to shout to each other. The French Canadian was silenced on his platform. His lengthy printed speech whirred decoratively in his hand. His curious mouth made interesting shapes in the air like a cooky cutter. And the sun shone hard upon everything. Quinn could see down the far slope of the bridge to the town of St. Ignace and beyond to the forests of the Upper Peninsula. Then Stanton found the liquor and the box lunches and they sat down. Quinn was hungry. Janey asked for the first time if they could go home now please, that is back to the club please, she didn't, if no one minded, want to go to jail. She was ignored by Stanton, and Quinn didn't know what to say to her. The players can't be expected to talk to the spectators.

"Have you served your country?" Stanton asked, indicating Quinn with the point of his sandwich.

"No," Quinn said, "I take, take, take and never give."

"Never been in the army?" Stanton knew he hadn't.

"No, have you?" Quinn knew that Stanton had been, of course. But it was expected that he should let Stanton rehearse this obsession.

"Just a little. I was found unfit for general consumption. Whenever I was in the barracks with a crowd of soldiers, my blood pressure climbed so high it distorted my vision. They had to let me go. Military hearts were broken. I couldn't see, Mr. Quinn, I couldn't see."

They tried to talk about other things, but Stanton smothered any incipient conversation not related to the trial he seemed to be conducting.

"I think they're starting to move," said Janey. She was looking out of the back of the bus. Quinn tried to see. "Wait, he's going on with the speech. This is our chance."

"No," said Stanton. Quinn wanted to get out too. He would even have agreed to run for it; but at the same time—and this is where he began to feel it—he recognized that there was something to be lost or recorded depending upon who first moved to escape. So he vacillated between numbing himself to their peril and searching the group outside for signs of restiveness. Looking at those faces beyond the window, he thought of stampede. "Why don't we bust open some of these other lunches?" he said.

"*Why don't we get out of here?*" Janey asked. The two men stared at her with disapproval. Stanton asked if she was complaining about the food and she told him that he wasn't funny. He reminded her that it was free and nourishing too. Quinn asked, "Anybody want any more —what is this?—pâté?"

"*Please.*" She hid her face, then uncovered it quite suddenly to say angrily, "I'm scared!" Quinn was unconvinced by this and wondered for the first time if she was in it too.

The floor was littered with sandwich wrappers and Stanton had thrown food. Ice cubes stood in small pools of melted water on the rubber aisle mat. Through the tinted windows of the Greyhound, Quinn could see lake gulls wheeling and screaming. He looked again toward the audience where G. Mennen Williams of the soap industry had replaced the French Canadian. The governor stood at the podium, his head turned to his predecessor. The Frenchman's eyes were directed toward the governor's bow tie, admiring its spotted surface. The governor looked at the Frenchman's hairline. All the mouths of the audience opened and closed in cries of spasmodic, unhearable laughter. The governor allowed himself a grin. Behind the podium the cars of the queens were parked in a semicircle and all of the queens huddled together for warmth and opened their mouths to laugh as the others did.

"Please please please."

"All right, *can* it!"

"For someone who was in the army such a short time," she said miserably, "you picked up so many of the expressions."

"Quinn, we live in a world wracked with strife."

"They're starting to move!" Janey cried.

"They've stopped again," said Quinn, making a grandstand play. Janey looked at him with surprise and disappointment. Before she could say anything, and Quinn dreaded what it would be, two women in wind-damaged picture hats stepped onto the front of the bus. Quinn thought this must be the end.

"We're not ready for you yet, ladies!" Stanton called; any reservations Quinn had fell away, and the admiration flooded in. When he glimpsed Janey, he saw that her eyes too reflected an unexpected pleasure. The two women retreated, Quinn supposed for reinforcements; they didn't look as if they had been taken in. Stanton, meanwhile, was talking about a plan he had for raising a Mormon shipwreck off Beaver Island. But Quinn allowed his eyes to fasten upon the door in a point-sacrificing manner; therefore, he was the first to descry the entrance of three gentlemen of the order of Shriners. They all three wore the headgear of their fraternity, the fez. Stout gentlemen, they suggested that Shriner life suited them to a T. Visible behind them were the two women who had appeared earlier.

"*Say!*" said the first of the gentlemen in the fezzes. His face had gone beef red at the sight of the three and the *untidiness* which they had created.

"Out out out," said Stanton, hurrying the first gentleman, and in turn the others, by pushing his chest. "Not another word if you're going to thrust yourselves in here like that. *Not one more word.*" He pushed them out the door, shut it with a rubbery clatter and returned.

Quinn was awestruck. He wanted Stanton's signature on his infielder's mitt. Stanton went on about his shipwreck. He said it was a small steamer and was carrying a printing press. A multitude looked in the windows of the bus. "Shall I open another box lunch?" Quinn asked, trying to regain his self-respect in the face of Stanton's tour de force. But he saw only the commonplaceness of his suggestion reflected in Stanton's eyes.

"I'm full, thank you," Stanton said. Quinn was ashamed of himself. He should have refused to play; but now that he was, he was ashamed for playing so poorly. How could he become a tycoon and a savant or even tell people what to do when he behaved like this? People were pounding on the windows. "Let's get the show on the road," Stanton said and walked forward to the door. The three gentlemen of the fraternal order were standing just outside. They had been joined by the lieutenant-governor and by the smoked pickerel queen who had lost her elusive prettiness in indignation. Stanton opened the door and looked upon them like a censorious bishop. "What is it?" He had become this bishop. "Yes?"

"Look, you!" It was the first Shriner once more, his fez drolly askew.

"Do you have tickets?" Stanton asked. He was stern with these people.

A roar: *"Tickets!"*

Stanton closed the door and latched it. Quinn could feel nothing around him. He floated in his seat. Stanton pulled down the microphone and held its button. His voice was loud outside as he spoke. *"Regular bus service begins—"* here he consulted his watch *"—in about thirteen months. Now I know that's a long wait and I would like to suggest to those of you who didn't bring just an awful lot of camping equipment that you spend the interim building shelters of a simple, utilitarian kind and gathering essential foodstuffs."* He released the button, replaced the microphone and drove away. When the shouting of the canaille died behind, there was only Quinn's helpless, rueful applause.

Stanton hired an off-duty patrolman to deliver the bus to the Otsego County grange hall for their annual VFW picnic. The officer hesitated until Stanton hinted that there would be something in it for him at the other end. "Keep money in front of these bozos if you want action." They went to the boat where Stanton popped the tarp off its grommets and gathered it in his arms to stow belowdecks. Quinn lent a hand, trying to size up Stanton's intentions. Stanton opened the hatches and ran the ventilation blowers before starting the engines. They cast off, reversed out of the slip and moved toward the bridge steadily. When they drew under it, Stanton shifted the engines into neutral and got out the glasses. Directly above them, the crowd they had just left straggled south toward Mackinac City. "We bitched them good," said Stanton, pushing the outermost levers forward. The yacht began to move again on the brilliant chop. Stanton pulled up the hinged seat in front of the controls, fixed its support rod and sat down. Quinn leaned against the shelf under the windshield, seeing over the front of the boat the flat breaking of water at the bows. The deck tapered forward with its narrow consecutive planks of holystoned teak; and on this surface, like some sculptural display, were the polished horns and big knuckled-over searchlights.

"Janey isn't fond of boats, are you?"

"Not very."

"And since she is a social do-gooder, she figures it's childish to have such expensive playthings. Is that accurate?"

"Pretty much."

"I once recommended Janey to Clara Barton, founder of the Red Cross Rescue Relief. I said here is a girl who can rescue and relieve. James, old sport, I've had the boredom around my neck more than once and I haven't been ashamed to scream. I screamed like a Bedouin. What's the matter with me, Mr. Quinn. I have what men dream of. I'm free, white and twenty-one with sixty zillion dollars billowing in a green cloud out of my asshole and I am obliged to scream like a Bedouin. Explain that to me, Cedric, and I'll buy you a new Slazenger."

"I can't explain."

"It comes up around my throat like a cold ring and I find I am a pagan with less energy than an odalisque and there is no God. Why?" Quinn thought of the tooth that had floated out of his tongue.

"I don't know. I can't explain it."

"If God will show himself, I will buy *him* a new Slazenger." They drove leisurely in the boat that rolled along at the cost of fifty-six gallons an hour. Stanton continued to introduce the usual topics: the Dreyfus Affair, the Papist conspiracy in America, the eruptions of Popocatepetl, Shakespeare, the Monomoy Indians, freeze-dried food, jai alai. Suddenly he shook Quinn's hand. "Help me," he said, "I need your help. No tips, please. Women will not wear shorts or halters in town. I need your assistance."

"He drinks, he swarms . . ."

They were still a distance from the bridge at this point and Stanton swung the boat back in a sharp bank that was a reply to Janey. When they were a short distance from the bridge, Stanton cut the engines. The boat continued to drift, swinging slowly sideways. Stanton hurried below and came up with a megaphone, thrusting it out to Quinn's vision. As they glided now, turning sideways toward the bridge, he lifted a pair of binoculars to his eyes, hung them around his neck, raised the megaphone and called, *"What's the trouble? What are you walking for, you people?"* The crowd overhead was distant, silhouetted against the gibbous, china sky. Answering voices came but couldn't be made out. *"I can't hear you!"* Stanton called and the indistinct voices came again. The group above had stopped and looked down at them. *"Look, take my advice: regular bus service begins in thirteen months; stay where you are!"* A speck appeared against the sky, enlarging very rapidly to splash beside the boat, disappear and bob up again, a lady's shoe. Stanton contemplated it. "Ah, well," he said, tired. He threw the megaphone down the companionway and started the engines, which once again began their heavy, fuel-devouring drone.

Years had passed since they were here together. As boys, they had lived for such trips. The last one had been ruined by the oppressive and ridiculous presence of Stanton's father who wandered over the property with hunched, lugubrious shoulders, stopping people on paths, people with fishing rods and picnic lunches, to tell them what an ungrateful handful his son was; what a nasty little ingrate, his mother chimed in, not to know what side of his bread the butter was on. Quinn remembered the gentlemen, the women too, stopping in their green sportsman's kingdom to consider a series of rhetorical questions put to them by the boozy couple. The strange fact was that because Stanton at seventeen stayed sober, the deteriorated pair felt he was trying to be superior, to be condescending. And until the time they threw him out of the house to go to college, they skulked around and drank on the sly.

Stanton nosed the boat to the front of the dock; then, reversing its engines so that a heavy churn of disturbed water revolved away and under the pilings, he swung the stern up snug and shut off the ignition. "The boat came in handy once. We made a fast exit from the El Convento Hotel in San Juan where I had been lewdly handled by Janey's Aunt Judy, who is younger than she is."

"Vernor, don't do that," Janey said.

"What were you escaping?" Quinn asked.

"Turpitude."

"Ah, then."

"This Aunt Judy was the love of my life, such as it is."

"We believe you, darling; but do shut up."

"No wantum to."

"Do anyway."

"I lived on the boat and made a regular appearance at the El Convento, walking up from the dock through San Juan memorably dressed in a white linen suit made for me in Martinique—"

"Why don't you stop talking, darling?"

"Because I am obliged to recognize the great pleasure that it brings to others. Anyhow, brilliantly attired in this suit and wearing a chest protector constructed entirely of Yankee dollars, I went to the El Convento where as a matter of ritual I blew fifteen hundred at chemin de fer and ascended to the third-floor workshop of my two lady friends."

"I'm not Cinderella."

"No, ma'am."

Janey said to Quinn, "In Vernor's simple world, women are either Cinderellas or professionals."

"That's right!" said Stanton happily. Janey looked at him.

"I am not either one," she said.

"My world is a horse opera. You know that. Where was I?" he asked Quinn.

"Going up the stairs."

"Okay, and it was a question of whether or not someone had gotten at Judy before I could get at her. I considered it a good week when I batted, so to speak, five hundred. It was usually much—" he cleared his throat "—worse. Nevertheless, I fell in love. And we had a dry-run honeymoon."

"Oh, Vernor, what's the point?"

He went on, "We sailed away, away, over the sea. Judy and Vernor. Hearts and flowers. Away. The moon rose in hugeness over the Caribbean with a single wind-bent palm courtesy of Eastman Kodak in the foreground. Judy and Vernor, somewhat closer in the foreground, scuffled hectically and made love like . . . *monsters*." He paused and said, "Oink."

"Do you want to see his vaccination?" Janey asked Quinn.

"No, but you're kind to offer."

"It didn't work out. Judy packed and left me and Janey in the hotel and we just got sort of real attached. Didn't we, sugar? Hm?—Oh, look, you're the one I love now! That was before, the monster stuff."

"You be the judge," she said. This seemed to make him nervous and Quinn therefore welcomed it.

"You're coming down a little hard, aren't you, darling? Where's your sense of humor?"

She lit another of her innumerable cigarettes, dragged on it, throwing the match away, and said, exhaling smoke, "No, you weren't trying to be funny, I guess." She waved the smoke away with the hand that held the cigarette.

Early the next morning, Stanton appeared in Quinn's doorway with a globe of iced orange juice which he put with a glass next to Quinn's bed. "The first Bug House party is tonight," he said. "There'd be no living here if we missed it."

"Thanks," Quinn said, pointing at the juice. He poured a glassful of it. "Yes, I'll go."

"All the old turds have arrived for long stays too. Jensen, Fortescue, Spengler, both Van Duzens, Jaycox, Laidlaw, Scott. All the people that hate us."

"Okay, I'll go."

"I'm glad you're willing. This is now my residence and I'm afraid it will need a little softening up before it's much of a place to live in." Quinn stiffened. "That's where you would be some help to me." Quinn thought that this must be the measure of how thoroughly he had succumbed at the bridge yesterday: Stanton's consideration of him as an automatic accomplice was restored.

Stanton lit a cigarette, looked upward and blew white smoke into the morning sun. "Why don't you cut out this business baloney?" he asked. Quinn didn't want to answer. He was susceptible and he didn't want ridicule.

"Because I like it," he answered anyway.

"You love it."

"I like it. A lot."

"Hire a manager, why don't you, and join me in making the world tense. We'll foment discord."

"That was before. Besides, you're a married man now."

"Not so," said Stanton, "Janey won't marry me."

"She won't?" asked Quinn lamely.

"Under your hat. We get wedding presents."

"Why won't she marry you?" This embarrassed Stanton.

"Says I'm too mean and crazy. She says she's sorry she loves me and I don't blame her. I think it's bad luck for her too. I'm not domestic."

By the time Stanton left, it was almost noon. Quinn made himself lunch and got his fishing gear together and went to the river above the woodcock marsh. It was too bright. His floating line threw a beaded shadow along the bottom; and though Quinn worked hard for nearly an hour and a half and until his eyes ached from the concentration, he failed to raise a single fish. He put on his Polaroid glasses and kept wading until he came to a turning cutbank that terminated in a round, flowing pool, deep and alder-rimmed. Right away, he saw the silver, dull flashes of nymphing trout in its depths. He tried combination after combination on them without success until the perspiration ran off him. On a hunch, he tied on a small green nymph and caught four good rainbows in a row before he put the rest off their feed.

As he waded back, he saw that the sun had changed

its angle and the river had gone quite metallic. Quinn was suffering a not unusual loss of faith and believed that all the trout were in his creel, that the river held no more. He went back through the marshland hoping to put up a woodcock. Not a sign. Nothing flew or swam when his belief failed.

As he circled beneath the plateau the top of which was the compound, he heard the adult, braying voices of the deadly offspring of the founding generation. He remembered the party tonight.

Janey was on the porch. "Isn't Vernor with you?"

"He left before lunch," Quinn said, stripping off his waders and stepping into his shoes. Janey said that he must be in the gallery then. When Quinn asked if she wouldn't have heard him, she said that he wasn't going to shoot; he was going to make bullets out of some stained-glass-window lead he had bought: it had the right tin content or something. "Well, come in," Quinn said. "I have to clean these." He patted the creel. He pushed the wicker chair over by the entrance to the kitchen and Janey sat down. He handed her the issue of *Vogue* with the farting moon women and went in and put the three trout in the sink. He liked to see trout in a porcelain sink. He liked to see them on a newspaper almost as well, though not as much as the sink. It wasn't the same with game birds. A grouse bleeding on the newspaper could be disturbing, for example; while in the sink, it had the quality of rare foodstuff. Quinn picked up the largest fish, gripped it under the gill plates and opened it with his pen knife from the vent all the way up to the point of the lower jaw, detaching the gills there and at the base of the skull and pulling the entrails away in a piece. In the middle was the whitish translucent stomach and its dark contents showed through. Quinn split it carefully, spreading the insides with the blade of his knife on the porcelain: hundreds of undigested nymphs. The second, smaller trout contained the same plus a bright minnow and a few red ants, some of which had eaten into the stomach lining. There was one brown honeybee in the third. Quinn removed the dark blood along the spine of each fish because it made the meat bitter, rinsed them, wrapped them in wax paper and put them in the icebox.

"I'm nervous about tonight."

"It's nothing to worry about."

"Vernor said they do this every Saturday. But what do they do? The thing is, they must be so practiced up. I mean what goes on?"

"At the Bug House? Drink a lot. Talk about years past. It's sometimes touching and usually boring. The worst of it is the singing. The rest shouldn't bother you. But the singing can be a mudbath—" Quinn stopped. He had just found a packet of sixty or seventy business letters which, on quick examination, proved to be half junk mail. The covering letter from Mary Beth began, to his special disgust, "Dear Boss Man."

"When Vernor and I were kids, we listened in on those Bug House parties. We thought all that boozy talk was Roman oratory. But my mother hated the parties and wouldn't let me go near them when she could help it."

"Why did she hate them?" Janey asked, as if the point of view of another woman would make her see it.

"My father always stopped off there when he came up for weekends. And when he came in, still dressed in his sharkskin suit from the office, and his face was ballooning under a narrow-brimmed Borsolino, she knew that he was in no condition, as they say. Sometimes he brought his pals and they drank and crashed around and cried and sent my mother fluttering upstairs to polish her driftwood collection. And you should have seen the stuff; it all shone like agate."

Janey kept asking questions. She couldn't imagine that someone who had known Stanton as long as Quinn had, worked; and she asked how his father had come to give him his business and when. "All right," he said. He liked the story. He told how his father had discussed arrangements on the golf course. The prospect of retiring had upset him so much, he drove the electric cart recklessly and finally turned it over, breaking his leg in three places. Quinn stood next to him, helpless to remove the thousand-pound cart upside down on his father's legs. A greenskeeper tried to help and tipped the cart up halfway before dropping it back on his father, who brought the ambitious idiot to earth with a single blow of his Cary Middlecoff weighted brass putter. Eventually, they loaded his father, fussy and upset as a baby, into a sod wagon drawn by a tractor and took him to the club-house and called an ambulance. Quinn was covered with spilt battery acid from the electric cart, and as he waited in the pro shop his Bermuda shorts melted off him, leaving him standing in ventilated underwear that was going very fast too. Quinn helped his father into the ambulance. His father's hair was filled with Kentucky blue-grass seed and shone like an aureole of gold. Quinn remembered his gasping from the stretcher, "And they call golf a sissy's game!" Afterward, when friends told stories of danger on the African veldt or the Guatemalan highlands, Quinn's father told a golf story and showed scars. He said no man needed to go to the wilderness.

Janey seemed amused by the account. She leaned on her hand, hiding her smiles. But then, when it passed, she looked off to one side, at nothing, the eyes slate and very clear, the straight nose, the mouth now slightly compressed, expressionless, vacant and fine.

"Have you ever hit Vernor?" she asked.

"No."

"Has he ever hit you?"

"Once."

"What for?"

"I said there was no God."

"I often think he's fairly crazy," she said. "Sometimes he talks such foolishness that I imagine him blowing up in front of my eyes. It doesn't seem you can talk crazy for so long and stay in one piece." Strange how apt this seemed to Quinn. He saw how she must have her hands full with Stanton, helping him while he vilified her publicly, then swamped her with affection. Quinn had the same sense she had that Stanton held some unfathomable capacity for wrecking himself. He might very well blow apart, as Janey thought, doing it as he would in his unique way, but exploding still, a nova, as Quinn imagined, blazing arms, legs, torso, head, away from the center, each part trailing flames in the sky, the head raving in a military fashion: now hear this, can it, the order of the day is that an army at rest will not profit, Napoleon did not profit, mount up men and get the show on the road as I am losing my head, my mistress, my bank account, my charm, my hair. Quinn thought of Janey trying to contain this corrosive silliness and she seemed so much in danger that he thought of himself as the rescuer. She lit a cigarette, inhaled and then exhaled as though trying to get the smoke away from her. She moved her seat out of the direct afternoon sun slanting across the room from the tall rolled-glass windows that were violet from years of strong light.

"Well, I hope you still like him," she said.

"Can't you tell I do?"

"Not really, no. I guess I had a different idea of things. Vernor talked about you all the time. Then when you were, I don't know, cold to him . . ." She couldn't have been expected to understand. And though it bothered him to have given such an impression, he knew Stanton would remember and get it right. Quinn's refusal to cooperate with Stanton had a number of sides. Quinn knew that if you played patty cake with Stanton he would soon be all over you.

Quinn hung back. He could see the green compound on its ineffable mound darkening in the evening. He could see the trees merge to a dark wall around the compound and the sky deepen above it. He could hear many a silly voice. In the compound the Bug House glowed yellow and hummed like a hive, and even at this distance he could hear the screen door clatter as another club member went in. He could see the people inside, a dark moving spot in the center of the surrounding screened light like the yolk of an egg. He went forward. He went back. He wondered if a grotesque fuss were to be made of him. Supercilious questions about his long absence. He pressed his hair down on top with the flat of his hand, adjusted his silk ascot, ran his thumb behind the lapels of his jacket and stepped out of the bushes. Leaving his house, he had felt suitably dressed, his outfit comfortably integrated; by now, however, he felt ensnared in his clothes, as though he might have to slash his way out. He walked toward the Bug House and could hear the sounds of the night, the frogs chirping below, the steady woodland throb of the generator. The Bug House with its light was a tall oval in the night and delicate barn swallows dove through the tapering top after armored bugs that were the color of varnish. Overhead, you could feel rain hanging in the warmth of the night; and Quinn knew that there would be hatches of insects and good fishing if he could get to it.

"The true Quinn!" yelled Stanton in an opening bid, as Quinn entered briskly. "I feel certain that he can tell you." Five faces turned to the door quizzically. Quinn knew them all right. "Tell how you touched down in that crop-dusting plane and tore up a hundred yards of turnip seedlings." Quinn pulled the door shut behind him, perplexed at having to whip something together so soon. Janey leaned in repose on the piano beside Stanton. Quinn wondered what fatality obliged him to continue. The five had moved around him and he addressed himself to them.

"Picture me," he said, "in my Steerman biplane dusting

away, as it were. Suddenly, I touch down and tear up a hundred yards of turnip seedlings." This seemed a suitably inane place to stop. Stanton was delighted. One of the five coughed.

"Tell them what happened when you returned to the airport many months later," said Stanton slithering onto the piano. This would be difficult to play.

"Many months later," Quinn began, ransacking his brain.

"When you returned to the airport—" One of the five, Fortescue by name, assisted.

"That's right, and the Steerman biplane had been left neglected out in the field. I couldn't find it. 'Where's my Steerman biplane?' I asked a farmer. 'Out there,' he said. 'Out where?' 'Out there in the turnip patch.'" Quinn considered this merely an escape maneuver; but Stanton was much affected. He fell off the piano, for one thing, and could be heard more or less barking from the floor. Quinn went over to the table and made himself a drink. Purely on the basis of Stanton's response, he awarded himself a certain number of points. He looked around. The five were still standing, not having yet broken the crescent they had formed. Then, two at the right end, Sturtevant and Olds, looked at each other and began to move. This precipitated a general movement among the others who, yes, they were beginning to move now, mostly just turning in their tracks, but there was sign of life here, the play of expression on the faces like shadows on glass; and before long they had become part of the crowd of thirty who talked and leaned into each other's smoke. Quinn joined them and ingratiated himself by starting up a conversation with Fortescue about his collection of military miniatures, the largest in the country. ". . . my point being," Fortescue concluded, "that such quantities of horse are scarcely imaginable at Ypres—" he was talking about a competitors' collection "—and therefore this fool had made the whole battle implausible to me. I don't expect perfection. After all, I have displayed hussars with paint bubbles on their chests and artillerymen divided by the seams of sloppy casting. But I find a historical lapse like this abhorrent." Quinn said that he was putting it mildly.

Meanwhile, another member named Scott, an obsequious professor to whom the academic life had given an avid taste for the outside world, greeted everyone who came through the screen door—many were entering for the third and fourth time—with the phrase, "Nice to see you." Quinn's main fear all along was Stanton and that is why he buried himself in this group. Spengler, the chronicler of the club, was explaining his race against time to finish his account of the club's first hundred years by the centennial on the Fourth. "Nice to see you," said Scott, looking past them with his diluted eyes. There were under twenty-five hairs in his moustache. "My account," said Spengler, "is very thorough and does not quail before realities."

"Nice to see you."

"Where have you gotten your information?" Quinn asked.

"Letters and diaries mostly. There was an early account, done around the turn of the century, which I take issue with. This was written by a local boy who resented the club and who was not a member. The name of his account was *Hellfire in the Woods* and tried to prove that the club was founded for disreputable reasons. I take issue, Quinn."

"Nice to see you, Bob."

"As well you should," said Quinn. He could see Stanton craning his neck. He was after Quinn.

"And I put it right on the line. Everybody asks me if I am afraid to write my chronicle before I see what is in the time capsule and I answer that thorough research has no fears. The thing is this, the first ten years are terra incognita and my job is to reconstruct them. I do not quail, Quinn." Stanton had the scent now. He was moving. Quinn's stomach got colder.

"Nice to see you."

Olson came in. Thin, intelligent Jack Olson, native of this Northern country, was wearing an apron and carrying a tray, holding the tray aloft on his left hand and with the other unloading snacks, bonbons and party favors. As Stanton went in one end of the group, Quinn squeezed out the other and went over to Olson. "Why aren't you fishing?" Olson asked. Quinn liked the quiet sanity of his voice.

"I don't know why," he confessed.

"The big duns will be on the water. I got a handful of nymphs out of the feeder creek and the shuck was all dark, almost black on the top where the wings show. Why don't you pass this up?" Olson said contemptuously of the party. He knew Quinn wouldn't misunderstand him.

"What about you?"

"Tell you what, I'll have a look at the river. If I got it right about the hatch, I'll come get you."

"That'd be good. I'd love to go. What about Vernor?" Olson looked over at Stanton who made his way from conversation to conversation toward them. He didn't conceal the hesitation before saying, "Why not." Quinn nodded, then turned hopelessly back toward the group to find Stanton opposite him, having sandwiched some of the older members between himself and the unwitting Quinn. He was encouraging them in sentimental reminiscence. "Autumn boulevards," he was saying. "A leaf falls slowly to the sidewalk, right?"

"That's what happens," said an old gentleman sadly.

"How about when you first found that old portrait of Mummy in her wedding gown?" Assenting murmurs. "And the portrait is in an oval frame?" More of them. "Now, what about this: the summer house is boarded up. The luggage is out on the porch. The refreshment stand is closed for the winter. Already, the ocean just isn't as blue—"

"Oh, gawd!" said one of the women morosely. Stanton seized the moment to begin singing softly and in the most cloying voice possible, *"Should auld acquaintance be forgot*—Come on, won't you join me, fellows!" The others, staring and unwilling, began. Stanton stopped them priggishly. Quinn saw Janey a short distance away, watching and talking to no one. By this time, Stanton had gathered most of them in front of the piano. He was running back and forth with a purely imaginary choirmaster's scuttle, adjusting shoulders and making people stand up straight. The others began to look on. "Come, ladies!" Stanton cried joyously. "You join us, too, won't you?" Some of the women who had stood aside piled in behind. "James!" he called, letting his eye fall horribly on Quinn. "Do us the honors on the piano!"

"No, I—"

"James!" The contemptuous disappointment that Quinn had seen when he offered the box lunches at Mackinac began to spread on Stanton's face.

"I may as well," Quinn said, overpowered. Stanton bent to the storage box beside the bandstand. He stood up with a tuberous, corroded saxophone in his hands, the reed of which he inspected earnestly. He pulled up a folding chair next to the piano where Quinn was now seated and sat down. Quinn watched his useless fingering of the rigid keys. "Now! On three, you all begin to sing and Quinn and I begin to play!"

"Sing what!" any number of people asked at once, and angrily too. They were not happy with this.

"Cut it out! 'Auld Lang Syne'!" Quinn experimented with the piano. He spread his fingers as he had seen others do and pressed to see if it would be a chord. It was not. Part of the choir looked over, brows furrowed. Quinn stood up halfway from the bench, laughed and sat down again. "All right now! Here we go! And a one and a two and a THREE." He put the end of the saxophone in his mouth and honked it terrifically (*Phnoo!*) as the singing began, "*Should Auld Ac—*" and Quinn splashed his hands into the keys, looking up as the singing stopped on a miasma of unlikable groans and nasal flutings. Janey walked thin-lipped out the door. Someone said, "Most amusing" as the group broke up. Stanton said,

"Go then!" and the party was soon back to normal. Quinn looked over his piano at Stanton looking over his saxophone at him. "Janey's gone," Quinn said. He got up.

"You notice every move she makes, don't you, cowboy?"

"Each and every one."

"Isn't this a gang of spoilsports?"

"A gang."

"Janey won't like us for what we've done."

"I don't blame her," Quinn said. "We go too far."

"We have a history of that."

"Do we ever."

"I cherish that history, James. Cherish, do you hear me?"

"I don't intend to let it continue. I may as well say that. I don't intend to lapse again," Quinn tried to say conclusively. Stanton laughed.

"Janey thinks that hope lies in your reforming me. I told her that that was a good one all right."

"I don't see why that has to be ridiculous."

"It's ridiculous because you're childish."

"Am not."

"Are so."

Into Quinn's head flashed a view of himself before an emergency meeting of the board. A lady from Flint who had formed a controlling coalition of minor stockholders was accusing him of childishness. *"J'accuse!"* she cried from under her net-covered birdscape hat. *"J'accuse!"* His father was among the figures at the meeting, fabulously corpulent, employing two chairs to keep his memorable behind off the boardroom floor. His refrain was

"Flagrant neglect!" and it was sung counterpoint to
"*J'accuse!*"

"*J'accuse!*"

"Flagrant neglect!"

"*J'accuse!*"

"Flagrant neglect!"

His father was wearing a flat West Indian planter's
hat and smoked oval cigarettes in a burnished pewter
holder. He sat next to the lady from Flint, in Quinn's
mind, and tormented Quinn until he no longer cultivated
the fantasy. Instead, he worried about his absence and
about the moist wads of business letters that seemed to
pertain to small problems but which may have been the
insinuations of vast financial cancers. Only gradually did
his mind return to the party which had become quieter
and less ridiculous than he had planned. In fact, he and
Stanton were the only ridiculous elements in it. All
around, darkness enclosed the screen wall, though the
yellow interior light was happy and reassuring. Moths
and flying beetles beat against the screens and bounced
away to beat again in an irregular guitarlike sound. Quinn
looked over at Stanton who had rested his chin on the
piano, a cigarette in his lips that stretched out perpendicular to the piano's surface. One of his hands, held invisible, pecked out "Clair de Lune" falteringly. He sang
a few lines of the song around the wobbling cigarette,
without lifting his head from the piano or removing the
cigarette; and now he smiled out at his imaginary audience, his great teeth locking the long white cigarette
horizontally. The glow of its end was reflected on the
surface of the piano until the ash fell and obscured it.

Quinn was touched from behind. He turned. It was Jack Olson more familiarly dressed in faded work clothes and loggers' shoes. He confirmed his prediction about the fishing. Quinn put his drink down and looked around to see if he'd left anything. Olson checked again if Stanton were still coming and Quinn nodded and waved him over. Stanton advanced, placing one foot before the other. Quinn explained about the hatch and they agreed to change into waders and meet back of the main lodge.

Fifteen minutes later, Quinn and Olson stood waiting for Stanton. Even on high ground the air was full of duns settling into the trees to oxidize and mature. Olson was switching his rod back and forth and shaking his head; angry, probably, asking himself why he had gotten involved. Olson was a serious sportsman, with rigid and admirable ideas of sporting demeanor. He managed the club, Quinn knew, to put himself onto its thousands of private acres which he had poached all through his youth and continued, more conveniently, to poach as a man.

Quinn knew Olson's study of problems natural to the taking of trout and bringing grouse to the gun had made him so knowing a woodsman that many of the members whose forebears had formed the association resented him. Quinn had more than once seen their reproachful glimpses of Olson's old Heddon rod as they unloaded the two-hundred-dollar magic wands from fitted leather cases. They didn't like the way he shot his brace of partridge out of their woods on his day off and they didn't like the way he did it over a scruffy working Springer when all their professionally trained Llewellyns, Weimaraners,

German Shorthairs, Labradors, Chesapeakes, Goldens and Wirehaired Pointing Griffins ran deer, flushed birds two miles from the gun or collapsed from overeating. During the annual meeting at the Book-Cadillac Hotel, there was always a discussion of whether or not to charge Olson dues. What sustained this annual joke was definitely not its humor; and there were members who weren't trying to be funny and who regarded Olson as an impudent interloper.

None of this quite got back to Olson. The membership well knew that any hint of it and he'd be gone. No one could replace him. His years of poaching on club property gave him knowledge of it all. He knew where salt licks had to go, what crop had to grow in the open valleys and when it had to be knocked down to make winter-feed for the game birds; he knew how to keep the lake from filling with weeds and reverting to swamp; he knew when herons and mergansers were glutting themselves with trout fry and had to be discreetly bumped off with his twenty-two Hornet; he understood completely how to intimidate professional poachers from the nearby towns who, if they found one chink in his mysterious armor, would run like locusts over the tote roads at night, shining deer with aircraft landing lights and spearing trout on the weed beds. A nest of eagles had been in use for a decade under his management, in spite of glory runs by members of local varsity clubs. The main lodge was calked and varnished at generous intervals; the Bug House screened and shingled. The lake maintained a good head of native-bred trout and the woods sang with life. All of this the Centennial Club got rather cheaply, considering. What they didn't like was Olson's primacy in the blood sports. They wanted to be the heroes and Olson made them look like buffoons when accident forced comparison. In short, they wanted to kill as he killed without the hard-earned ritual that made it sane. For Olson, hunting and fishing were forms of husbandry because he guaranteed the life of the country himself. When the members came swarming out of the woods with their guns and high-bred animals and empty hands to find Olson, with his unspeakable Springer spaniel at his feet, turning a pair of effortlessly collected grouse over a small bed of hardwood coals, or when they found him with a creel full of insect-fed trout and had to conceal the seven-inch mud-colored hatchery trout that looked more like a cheap cigar than a fish and that they had nearly smashed the two-hundred-dollar fly rod getting; when all that happened, they wanted to call the annual meeting right then and there and tell this interloper to get off the property before they got a cop. Then they remembered he was the manager and it became more complicated without changing its impulse.

With no apologizing, Stanton said, "Lead me to fish."

"Let's go," Olson said shortly. They started down. All three men had flashlights and played them about the path at their feet that sloped down to one end of the woodcock marsh. The duns now seemed to hang in the air like gauze and Quinn continually brushed them away from his face and hair, squinting downward to the small disc of light that skimmed the path in front of him. Stanton hung back until Olson was well in front and whispered to Quinn, "Is Herr Olson impatient with me?"

"*I* was impatient with you."

"Mister Quinn, I never wear my Bug House clothes to the river." Quinn noticed Stanton's multi-pocket vest and brush pants in the penumbra of his flashlight. They went on down as the angle of the path's decline began to flatten out and they could feel the coolness of the low ground rising about their legs. Quinn heard Stanton behind him swear to himself bitterly. In front of them now, the river rattled in its hard bed. "Vernor," said Olson at the bank, "why don't you wade up to the rollway pool from here. Stay to this shore and you will have hard gravel all the way. When you can't hear the river running so hard you'll know you're at the pool."

"I know where the pool is," Stanton said.

"Okay. What fly have you got on?"

"Let me worry about that. Goodbye. I'll meet you back here." Stanton got in the river. The pines at the far side were completely black; the sky above lighter and the river below a sheen, also lighter. Stanton soon disappeared but they could hear him wading, a deeper note than the river made without him. Olson turned to Quinn. His green suit made everything but his face disappear. It seemed to float, rounder because his hair was thinning.

"Why don't you drop down a ways and fish the off bank back to here," he said. "You know the river."

"Fine with me."

"I'll fish below the creek outlet."

"I think you're giving me the break," Quinn said.

"Plenty of river for us all. Does Stanton know how to find that pool?"

"I think so."

"He knows all the answers, doesn't he?"

"You must make allowances," Quinn said.

"Shit too," said Olson. A sample of the talk that brought his name to the fore every year at the Book-Cadillac. "Anyway, catch a fish."

"I'll do my best."

Quinn got in the river and waded to the far bank where he knew the current had deposited enough gravel to leave a safe walking ledge. It was never comfortable wading at night though; he could see the water around his waist shine so that he knew where it was. But the sight of bottom that was so reassuring when wading in fast water was lost. As he waded, he switched out line from the end of his rod, working it gradually into the air. The big wind-resistant night fly was hard to move until he had thirty feet of line up and then it began to carry and hiss as it passed overhead. He began to fish automatically, taking his exercise, thinking. He was just beginning to be able to fish as he wanted to. It would always be a week until he could relax and bear down and fish with exactitude. But the hatch now was passing already. Too bad. Olson would feel responsible. The nighthawks that crossed back and forth above him were disappearing with the duns. Otherwise the spring uproar was at a peak, the forest as raucous as a one-man band. The river here was narrow with stable banks that let the trees grow close. Above his head they left a corridor of stars obscuring with streamers of cloud. Quinn knew Stanton was at the foot of his pool swearing and flogging water, wanting at any cost to come up with the best catch. Stanton was a competitive fisherman; that is, an odious apostate. He tried to beat fish out of the river. When successful, he challenged you with them. Olson who, as a fisherman, was his opposite number, fished deferentially and awaited his occasions. There were none of the streamside brawls between man and fish that grace the covers of the sporting periodicals. Olson had his unique alchemy and fished for sport. He kept only the fish he needed.

The sky had grown heavy and Quinn stopped casting and reeled up. The air seemed dense and he stood where he was and waited in the steady rush of water. The first thunder came and a hot seam of lightning opened across the southwestern sky. He knew it was dangerous to be in the river and he turned to wade back. Grape-size drops of rain started to fall and take the sheen off the river. He was dry only a moment more and then he was soaked through to his underwear. His hair clung to his skull. Unnerving drops ran down from the base of his neck and the sky overhead kept fracturing with livid fissures of light. He had to be careful going downstream. The tendency to trip on obstructions was increased with the current behind. When he could see Olson silhouetted on the far bank, he crossed over. Olson gave him a hand and he clambered up. They sat down and watched the river for Stanton. Olson had no fish either. Both men watched the sky, hoping the lightning would stay to the south and that Stanton would know enough to hurry. They waited another twenty minutes until the storm was tossing the tops of the trees and lightning was forking skeins of white light in the sky, then flashing afterward, soundless, like the retina of a camera. Stanton appeared on the far side and began to wade carelessly across, not strategically, but walking across the stream until, fifteen feet from their bank, he went down. Olson skidded in and told

Quinn to stay where he was. Quinn saw Stanton in the darkness, floundering and trying to get his feet under as Olson reached him. Their struggle made the water-reflected light shatter and curl away. They started again toward the bank, Stanton having maintained his fishing rod somehow; they went slowly and Quinn knew Stanton's waders held a tremendous weight of water. When he got to the bank, Quinn took the rod from him. He could hear Stanton's stertorous breathing. There was no hope of getting up the bank with the waders on and he had to shed them. Quinn helped him. Olson emptied the boots and flung them up on the bank and climbed out behind. "Give me some light, Jack," Stanton gasped. Olson turned on his flashlight and Stanton pulled up a heavy brown trout from his creel. He held it under the jaws and tail so that the butter-colored belly hung in a curve and all of the black and orange spots showed. "Take *that*," said Stanton with a wild and unexpected laugh. Olson was going.

"I'll see you boys in the morning," he said. He started up the path and soon was invisible to them.

"Is Olson miffed?" Stanton asked. "Or need I even ask?"

"We were damned nervous about the lightning."

"He was patronizing me, old Quinn."

"I don't think so. We were both pleased to see you picked up such a good fish."

"It is a good fish, isn't it. I'm not sure I remember seeing you *or* Herr Olson with such a trout, for all the celebrated expertise."

66

"That's right, Vernor. There has never been a fisherman like you."

They crossed the compound again. Quinn was determined to go back to his place, read and begin a program of avoiding Stanton. But there was still activity and the group had moved just outside the Bug House. Stanton and Quinn walked over. "Nice to see you," said Scott. There was a clamor as Stanton strutted with his trout aloft like a bullfighter with the ears of a bull. They were all gathered around a barrel of oysters that Spengler had flown in from Delaware. There was a basket of thin-skinned, almost translucent limes. Quinn borrowed one of the irons and a plate, then pried open a half dozen of the chalky, small oysters, revealing interiors as smooth as the inside of a skull. He squeezed lime over all of them and, lifting them one by one, sipped off the juice and with the surreptitious aid of his forefinger slipped each oyster from its moorings and into his mouth. Then he began again with the iron. He joined Stanton, carrying six new oysters. Stanton was talking to Fortescue who was once president of the club. Quinn had a better chance to observe him than he had had during their discussion of horse at Ypres. Fortescue wore military twill pants and an English hacking jacket; he had the face of a crazy spaniel. Quinn moved in to listen. Stanton was telling Fortescue that Jack Olson was trying to take over the club and turn it into a private shooting preserve. Quinn said, "That's not true." Stanton went red.

"Don't interfere, James. I won't pay dues to have him patronize me. He's done it before and now I want him drummed out of the corps. If Herr Olson wants to under-take contests, he has to take his chances."

"Patronizing you is not the same as taking over the club. I don't see why you equate them."

"Give him a step and he'll outflank you," said Fortescue. "It could be a feeler." Fortescue turned his right hand at an oblique angle to illustrate the flanking maneuver. He illustrated its effectiveness by holding the other hand supinely in place and allowing the right hand to flank it repeatedly, piling up advantages.

Quinn felt that something had to be said; but he knew he had sacrificed his position already by stringing along with the jokes that led up to this juncture. What made circumventing Stanton even trickier was the presence of some not quite visible plan which showed itself in Fortescue's cooperation. Short of the pieties of woodland life to which the club subscribed so heartily, nothing pleased them more than internecine strife. Stanton knew how to manage this impulse. In the episode with Olson, Quinn saw the beginnings of something catastrophic.

2

NATIVE
TENDENCIES

THE next day, after a flash of hatred had kept him awake through half the night, he settled into a state of contempt for Stanton's motives. He spent the morning expecting him to come down and had prepared a speech, sharply reprehending and corrective; but Stanton never came at all and Quinn's anger burned away, leaving him, by noontime, relaxed again and comfortable. After making himself a small meal, he decided he would take a long walk and went around the back of his house down the path with its coarse entanglement of peripheral vegetation. He came to a place where the path split up in six directions, scattering high and low through the woods. He halted, undecided, knowing what country each of these paths ran to but unable to decide which to take. So he resorted to sinistrality, the art or practice of turning left.

The first left turn took him below the cottage to a

piece of rich bottom land so round and low and free of heavy trees that it must recently have been water. The path skirted the lower end, bearing toward the river, and forked. Quinn turned left. This new path wandered about forty feet and swung up, intersecting the other branch; at the intersection, Quinn turned left and was back on the original path that soared up a brush slope, then glided down the other side into a long frog-roaring oval of standing water with its lid of pads and algae. Quinn went left around the perimeter and crossing its lower end sank halfway to his knees in black stinking muck that launched a cloud of mosquitoes up around his head. He slashed away at them until he regained the path on the other side and climbed a short distance, still striking at the mosquitoes so ineffectively that he could see four of them standing cloudily in his forevision, on one side of his nose. At the end of the last ascent, he was in a close but breezy deciduous woods, strolling on the firm ground wind-freed of insects, when he was confronted by an especially pointless path that went off through heavier going to the left. He hesitated, then took it, following no more than a rod when it opened on the end of a long, hotly sunlit paddock; at one end of it, Janey lay naked on her back in the smoky spring sun, her breathing slumbrous and regular. Quinn's eyes turned slowly, searching the clearing for Stanton; then his gaze settled upon her again lying in total female repose of lax unresisting limbs. She was below the level of breeze and not even her hair moved. The canyon of light above her was flaked and spinning with motes and insects, the trees too, everything, was in motion but her unmoving form stationed in his path as final as a landmine.

Then Quinn saw how he must get out of there, tumescence and all. There would be no explaining should she awake and find him rooted to the spot like a thief-proof cemetery marker. The retreat alarmed him as much as anything, the fear of her looking up in time to see him scuttling bushward, his polychrome mental picture safely fixed. But he was back on the main path, trudging along toward his cottage again, the brief experiment with sinistrality finished.

For the next two hours, he tried to read Thackeray's *Pendennis*, a volume from the sunbleached blue, uniform set that was the porch's only decoration. Even the weevil tunnel that penetrated Chapter One sent his mind hurtling back to Janey's bare-assed splendor.

Stanton arrived shortly after four and sat lazily on one of the porch chairs. Quinn upended the book in his lap, looked over and tried to remember his speech of reprehension and correction. Stanton was bored and fidgeting. Plainly, the last thing in his mind was Olson. So Quinn brought it up, asking him if he still planned to go through with his plan to have Olson removed.

"That's what I plan all right," said Stanton.

"I don't like it."

"Don't you?" said Stanton, bored. He stared at the screens. "Tell me this, what were you doing spying on Janey?"

"I wasn't spying on Janey. You'll have to make yourself clearer."

"She was sunbathing in the woods. You found her. You

must have been following." Quinn's heart pounded. He wondered if Stanton could see it. But how did Stanton know?

"All right. I stumbled on her out walking. And when I saw her, I turned around and went back the way I had come."

"That's not her version."

"What's her version?"

"She says you stood there about four hours with your mouth open."

"I'm not even going to answer you."

Stanton laughed then.

"I was kidding," he said, "she told it to me just like you say. And now may I ask a question?"

"What?"

"Isn't she some piece of ass? Don't answer that or I'll break your neck." He looked away with lazy, bored, intelligent eyes. "I have been figuring on exacting a price for this transgression."

This time Quinn watched the loading. The exquisite French pistols were to be used again. Stanton poured a charge and a half of ffg Peerless black powder into a graduated brass powder measure and transferred the charge by pouring it through a funnel into the muzzle of the first pistol. He did the same with the second as Quinn held the other upright in his hand and looked into the funnel as the silvery grains sank and vanished. Then Quinn held both pistols upright. Stanton unwrapped a small black cloth that had been twisted into a sack and held it out to Quinn. "Sure you wouldn't rather use these?" In the sack was a nest of perfect, round lead balls so new they were only slightly darkened with oxidation and each with a single shiny spot like the eye of a pea where the sprue had been cut. These must have been from the stained-glass-window lead. Quinn declined. They loaded the wax balls once again, which were more than sufficient to arouse Quinn's interest; the extra charge of powder promised the loser something.

Quinn did the counting as he rehearsed the two previous duels. He knew now that he had to turn, sight efficiently and quickly and without rushing, and squeeze off the shot. As he counted, he could feel the gun well fitted in his hand, hanging straight. His thumb and last three fingers were hard around the fluted grip and comfortable. His forefinger curved through the engraved and chased oval trigger guard, the slender, flat, polished trigger in the crevice of the first joint. Quinn knew the trigger was crisp and light, resisting then yielding like a breaking glass rod. All of it seemed, for once, understandable and controlled enough that at *Ten!* he turned, swung the long pistol up cleanly, the hammer cocked already to expose the sights, and fired. "Wowee!" cried Stanton. "I heard that one under my ear! Now, stay where you are. This is an affair of honor . . ." The shot rang metallically in the narrow gallery. Quinn fell. A sudden flood of dark red in his mind made him think he had been knocked unconscious. It was his throat this time. He was on the floor, choking there and trying to breathe. His wind seemed restricted to a channel the size of a pinpoint. It was only by violent fetching of his lungs that he enlarged this channel, millimeter by millimeter, until he could breathe again. He sat up, his face bathed in tears of pain, his legs splayed before him and, taking the slender pistol by the barrel in both hands, smashed it repeatedly on the floor until its beautiful, fluted stock and inlaid dragon locks were in pieces around him. He reached up and held his hands to his throat and saw Stanton, standing where he had been, serious, his pistol stuck in the top of his pants, hands plunged in his pockets, watching Quinn get up, look over at him again and mount the stairs. "I'm sorry, James," he said with unhappiness in his voice. "But I really can't let you pull that on the girl I love. How else could I make you understand?" Quinn didn't answer; he was sure he could not have. He felt a little more certain now that Stanton was a madman with unnatural power over him.

He only went as far as his porch. The pain in his throat was settled in one spot and throbbed. His feelings were hurt enough that, in his way, he wanted no retaliation. Stanton's unkindness seemed conclusive. He wished to put his mind off it and wondered if his voice was affected. He would say something. He picked up *Pendennis* and opened to the first page. He began to read aloud, "One fine morning in the full London season, Major Arthur Pendennis came over from his lodgings, according to his custom, to breakfast at a certain club in Pall Mall." The speaking soothed the bruised tissue of his throat. He read thirty pages more aloud, conscious of the silence around him, and found himself engrossed in the novel's progress. He read until dark.

When the sun fell, he went inside and put on a sweater. He turned on every light in every dark room. He made himself a whiskey and water, then gathered his letters from the office and answered each of them, clipping the answers to the originals and enclosing them in a manila envelope to return to Mary Beth for typing and sending. When he had done this, he had the illusion of a place in the outside world once more, a world untouched by the mania of boredom.

It turned cold during the night. In the morning he went out and was splitting kindling when Janey came. She wore a heavy blue sweater and narrowed her shoulders in the chill. She struck her hands together and shivered. Quinn said, "Is it that cold?"

"It is to me. I'm not chopping wood." Quinn wondered what she wanted; she came from his house. He put up the axe.

"How are you?" he asked.

"*I'm* fine. What about you? Vernor said you got . . . plugged."

"That's right."

"How terrible that must be. Can we go in? I'm cold. Or would you mind?"

"I would mind."

"But why?"

"I don't want to inspire Vernor to some new feat of aggression."

"Yes? Well, he'll be along soon."

"Say it isn't so."

She ignored his sarcasm.

"You smashed that French pistol—" she said.

"Sure did."

"It was worth a lot, you know."

"It was worth a lot to me smashed."

"I suppose. But it was a pair, you know, hundreds of years old. Can I go in and you stay outside?"

"No."

"Why?"

"Because to Vernor it will be indisputable evidence that I have just seduced you and have run out to clear my head."

"You know, he's not a lunatic."

"How can you tell?"

She didn't answer. Her pretty face became pretty in another way and she was now indifferent again and splendidly vacant. Only her energy betrayed the impression. "You surely get a two-bit spring in Michigan," she said distantly, "not that I intend to see another."

A moment later, Quinn blurted in unreasonable disconnection, "You realize, don't you, that I know you're not married?" But Stanton came before she could reply. He clowned up the path, improvising a little dance of pathos and hopeful apology. "The throat?"

"Sore."

"Next time we'll use milder loads and a little cheaper grade of pistol."

"You will discover that that was the last time I'll be going for the dueling."

"You think so?" The apologetic tone was gone. "Well, okay. Number two in the batting box is the matter of Olson. How do you advise?" Now he was actually turning the knife.

"I advise you to drop it."

"We're beyond that now. Reality comes to bear. The turning of wheels. Fortescue came by my place. He says

I hit on an ideal time to let Olson go. Summertime is strictly housekeeping around here. We can get a temporary until we find someone to do Olson's job."

"You won't find anybody who will do it as well as he can."

"Well, there again, we may have hit on a plan. You know how honest and thoroughgoing he is—" Quinn agreed. "Well, I hit on the idea of letting him suggest or even hire his successor. I mean, that strikes me as honorable."

"Why don't you try this for honor: why don't you go discuss this plan with him before you make another move?"

"We're talking about an employee, old pal."

"I know who we're talking about."

"All right. I'll do it. But let me pick the moment."

When they were gone, Quinn started on an angry cross-country hike to the west. He had to have a neutral corner. Shortly after he left the old club boundaries, he was out of the woods, on newer acquisition, cleared ground. This was the first of the farms now owned by the Centennial Club and represented the steady encroachment upon the lands of people whose antecedents had been expelled from the original grounds. He walked in the deep weeds toward the house, with meadowlarks and the small June grasshoppers showering around him. He could see the barn now. In this country unpainted wood weathered almost black. The barn doors had collapsed forward and lay out flat from the entrance which from this distance was only an oblong hole of darkness; swallows poured from it incessantly like smoke. The front

79

door was unlocked and he went in. Shattered glass in quantity and empty sky-filled window frames; nests were cemented into every crevice. The frequent entrances and exits of the birds were like the pluckings of a stretched rubber band. In the kitchen was an infantryman's jacket with a long column of World War Two duty stripes of the European theater. He went outside. In the southwest corner was a wasp's nest the size of a medicine ball; under its entrance five or six wasps hung as if in suspension. He wondered if the name of the former tenant would mean anything to him. When farmers hereabout went broke, the club served as a way station where, badly paid, they awaited jobs in Detroit. A long list of names came to Quinn's mind. Half of the surnames were Olson and the bulk of these were related by marriage to the other half. Quinn wondered if Olson would end up in Detroit.

He woke up late the next morning, stiff from his hike; and because Stanton jumped into his head first off, he decided his holiday was in full decline. He slashed out from under the covers, got to his feet and, looking down at his white thin nude self, said, "I am Spider." It would be hard to say what he meant exactly. He hunted in his suitcase, stirring its contents like a stew, for his bathing suit, and found it but could not find his supporter. So he put on his suit without it and then found it impossible to accustom his parts to any one side of the cold, hard, dividing crotch. He cried, "No starch I said!" and reheated some coffee. While drinking it, he sought his bath clogs. They were gone too. He breathed through his teeth. These bath clogs had been his friends. In the end, he was obliged to put on hiking shoes without socks. They seemed odd. He found a towel without any trouble and headed for the lake.

The lake was blue and still and empty save for a single, double-ended rowboat, apparently adrift. Three men stood out at the end of the canoe dock, looking at the empty boat. They turned to look at Quinn as he arrived in his bathing suit, ready for a swim. His great shoes were loud on the hollow dock. They were Fortescue, the military man, Spengler, the historian, and Scott, the sometime investigator of seventeenth-century topics. "Wind get the boat?" Quinn asked.

"No," Spengler said, "Stanton."

"Stanton—?"

"He's skin-diving," said Scott in his sneeping Ohio voice. "Troubling the trout, disturbing the redds." He waited futilely for someone to ask him what redds were.

"What's he after?"

"Treasure." Suddenly, timorous Spengler burst out: "His jokes and his money and his—" There was a great moist gasp beneath their feet like the sighing of a dugong and then somber and hollow and unmistakably Stanton the voice came, "God's wounds!" Silence again. Spengler was sleekit, timorous. Off the end of the dock, in the undisturbed water, and only barely visible against the dark bottom, a wobbly, undulant anthropoid form shot away and disappeared in the depths.

"What more do we require?" sneeped Scott to Spengler, turning then to Fortescue. He emphasized the significance of his question by letting his mouth drop open and shifting his jaw to one side. "What more?" He had short teeth and he wrinkled his nose.

"He's pressing all right," said Fortescue, principally to Quinn. Quinn looked up wordlessly at this collector of military miniatures.

"He's not all bad," Quinn said, stringing along.

"We know that," Scott said correctively, cocking his jaw again as though now to receive a blow, squinting. "We also know that he wishes to destroy our club and that for which it stands."

"What are you getting at?" Quinn wanted his swim.

"What we're getting at," Fortescue began firmly, then came to so helpless a halt that Spengler had to recover.

"The point is we want to fire Olson but we want to know if that is part of Stanton's plan to destroy our club—"

"—and that for which it stands," Scott added.

"Why don't you really outfox him," said Quinn, "and keep Olson on."

"Don't give us that," said Scott's averted face, "we're on to it." At that moment, Stanton appeared in the anchored boat, head thrown back, one arm crooked behind his head, a grotesquely muscled merman, the sun standing in the water around him like blossoms, glittering and collecting toward the shore where it cooled and disappeared.

"There he is again," Spengler cried as though he'd wanted to grab a harpoon and jump into a whaleboat. His eyes were wide and his light hair swam nervously in the wind.

"The point is," Scott thrust in suddenly, another of his

academic surprise strategies, "that you seem to have a modicum of sense even if your *confrere* doesn't. You're the only possible mediator and we figure you're essentially on our team."

"Oh, no," Quinn said, "that's completely wrong. I'm afraid you misjudge me." Fortescue laughed his sanguine nobleman's war laugh.

"We've been outflanked," he said.

"Somewhat," Quinn said, "in any case."

"You're playing it real wrong," Spengler insisted.

"Oh, no," Quinn said in surprise. "You've got it all mixed up again. I'm not playing anything. *I'm on vacation.*"

"So are we!" enthused Fortescue, playing the good old sport. But in his eyes, so much like those of an unsuccessful spaniel, was something furtive. From the boat came the sound of Stanton imitating an air-raid siren. They all looked over. What appeared to be the head of an enormous pink baby was rising over the gunwale—Stanton's naked buttocks. Each of them, for his own reasons, was stunned by this gratuity. Quinn, sharply resisting his first impulse, admired Stanton's expertise in showing only his ass from such a lowslung craft. Nothing could have been more singular than the marionette-like rising of this fleshy dome from the rocking stage of the boat. But Quinn's memory was taking over.

"Jeepers Christmas," Spengler said. The others were talking and going off; Quinn didn't hear them. History had crowded his skull that instant and he could have cried. He sat down and dangled now shoeless feet in the chill water and watched trout fry dart through the flat green weed as Stanton coursed toward him on sharp strokes of the oars, his cathedral back making regular hydraulic movements forward and back. Presently, he was beside the dock, the double-ender still as though it had never moved.

"What are you doing?" Quinn had collected himself.

"Seeking treasure."

"You horrified them."

"Child's play. Get in. I found a wreck. Help me raise it and we split the take." Quinn climbed aboard and sat in one end. The boat settled unevenly; Stanton was in the middle seat. As he began to row toward the middle of the lake, Quinn felt the boat lift slightly with each stroke. A wake of bubbles poured from the stem and Quinn imagined he was an officer in a blue tricorn, a brass telescope clapped shut in his lap, rowed to a defeated vessel by a piratic mate; then distant cannon reports over a steamy green sea. Stanton swung the boat around a floating Clorox bottle, tethered at its handle by an anchor line. He uncoiled a rope from under the seat and tied one end to the bow cleat, then without putting on the aqualung or even the mask, dove over the side with one end of the rope into the clear water that allowed his progress to be followed into a bluish, bubbled distance where he shrank from sight. He was gone a full minute before he rocketed into view and blew free of the surface. "The bends!" He rolled over the side. He sat down, took a hold of the rope and pulled it taut. Quinn got his hands on it too and they began to haul. At first, the boat heaved over but Quinn moved to the high side and they hauled more slowly until gradually

Quinn began to feel something give and then let go altogether as they pulled, becoming only weight to be raised; they lifted hand over hand, no more than thirty feet of hard finished .rope when Stanton said it was enough and took two turns around the oar lock. "Move carefully now and have a look."

Quinn leaned over the side and saw, about eight feet below them, suspended in the clear and dimensionless water, a sleigh, a single-horse cutter, as delicate as a scroll, hanging by the thin rope tied between the high curling runners. Stanton said that he had had to leave the horse behind, the skeleton that is, of a small horse, all four legs fallen directly beneath and pointing behind, the skull stretched forward like an arrowhead, as though the horse had been drawing the sleigh. They towed the sleigh behind and the rope rubbed and ground upon the stern with unseen motions. When they got to shore, they beached the rowboat, waded out, untied the sleigh and, carrying it between them, brought it ashore, upright and streaming with water, to set it high in the sunlight and on the grass. It was perfect. It might have been put to use. Then Stanton sat upon its narrow seat and it slung a little with his weight. Quinn carefully got on beside him.

"This rather redeems me as a treasure hunter, what?" asked Stanton.

"How do you mean?"

"The Mormon boat I told you about was raised a century ago, a few hours after it sank."

"By who?"

"By its crew."

"What will you do with this?"

"Buy a horse for it. Run wild like some intolerably picturesque Ukrainian. You're invited. Bring sable coat."

"I won't be there at all."

"Probably not." He got to his feet. "More's the pity. Now I have an appointment with Herr Olson as per your suggestion."

"Do the right thing."

"I have my own ideas about what that is."

"You're hedging," said Quinn, seeing too late that the fears of Fortescue, Spengler and Scott might have been justified.

"I'm not hedging. I am not a germ. I am not a coward. I have every intention of comporting myself as a gentleman."

"Never mind the medieval stuff. Do the right thing."

"What is this? What are you, a Dominican friar?"

"You're hedging," Quinn interrupted; but Stanton went right on; he would not be dissuaded.

"We get all the correction and fun-spoiling from you but where is the fucking benediction? Where is it?"

"I don't know what I've done with it."

"No—"

"But I have it somewhere."

"You do not. You're in the service of my enemies, trying to spoil my innocent pleasures."

"Innocent pleasures."

"They are. I haven't nosed around your domestic arrangements the way you have mine. And I'll bet mine are comparatively innocent. I have a feeling you've got closets full of whips and black capes, all the deviationist impedimenta." Quinn didn't answer. He reached and touched one of the runners sweeping up in front of them; the runners pressed below into the heavy June grass that swept up the hill to the black trees, beyond which Quinn's house stood barely invisible. "What are you doing to me, Quinn?" Stanton wouldn't look at him.

"Not anything bad for you."

"This has been a disappointment," Stanton said. Quinn had forgotten what his serious voice was like. Free of irony, it seemed maybe less distinguished.

"We couldn't keep up the old thing. That was insanity. If you don't outgrow it, the world leaves you holding the bag."

"That's all very good, since you want to get philosophical, if the world is very good. But it's not. It's bad. However, with surprising common sense, the world is building the bombs it deserves, and until such a time as those bombs are used, I intend to treat it like the shit it is." The speech fell from Stanton's mouth phrase after phrase, in complete readiness. He meant it, evidently; but Quinn told him he didn't. This seemed to irritate Stanton profoundly and he wouldn't have said anything more, even if Scott hadn't come up the lakeshore and tried to slip by in his characteristically abject fashion. He saw himself seen and said, "What's that thing?"

"A one-horse open sleigh," Stanton said. "What in the hell does it look like."

"Oh, boy," said Scott. "*Oh, boy.*" He disappeared up the path.

"I've got to be rough with these buggers," Stanton said quite seriously. "Otherwise they run all over me and I have to drive them back with banknotes."

"The thing is, Vernor, this shouldn't have been a disappointment to you."

"No, God damn it, I know that, I'm not a moron; but you're sandbagging is the point. This time three years ago—"

"—We'd been jailed."

"*That's right.*" Stanton was downright truculent. Quinn started to make a speech about the life of work and its virtues and rewards; but it caught in his throat and left a vision of Detroit with its artifact buildings, one of which held his offices, slabs, markers, a poison sky and a river that stank and curled sipping at its perimeters— in fine, the last place in the world to send a friend or start a utopian colony. Unusable and contradictory thoughts filled Quinn's mind with almost physical duress as though his poor head were a golf ball which, slashed open, shows its severed rubber filaments snapping and racing about in confusion. Stanton climbed down and went on with what he was saying. "I want pleasure, do you hear me? And not necessarily at the expense of others, smart ass. I can carry all expenses personally. But God damn it, if I want to pack my colon with beluga caviar I don't want any cool, assessing stares from you. You helped get me into this a long time ago and now you don't like the consequences because you change horses every time you get sick of one and call it growing up. The man of business. And don't imagine I haven't noticed the exchange of brain waves between you and

Janey. I'm aware of these particular vapors—" he raised his wide hand quickly to prevent a reply. "Enough said. But I know you, Quinn. When you've got your nature up I wouldn't walk past you with a roast suckling pig for fear you'd violate it."

"Much less Janey," Quinn said. Nothing came of it though. Stanton went up. Quinn remained on the cutter, the antagonistic talk leaving him ragged. But they were two temperaments and there was nothing new in it. When they were young, Quinn simply wanted to be a sportsman of gentlemanly cast and had modeled himself on the old trout fishermen of the Catskills and Adirondacks, Hewitt and Gordon and LaBranche, who wore plus fours and rode carriages to their stretches on the Esopus or Beaverkill. He had tried to include Stanton; but all Stanton's heroes were Comanches and his sole pleasure was in raiding or terrorizing the cottages and their inhabitants. Quinn always ended putting his rod away and joining the reckless episodes, often finally leading them until it began to get out of hand and he and Stanton competed for the controls. It began when they were twelve or thirteen; it reached acute, maybe eloquent pitch in an end-over-end trip across a back country farm in an Oldsmobile Starfire, Quinn driving, Carl Perkins yelling *"Honey don't"* all the way from East St. Louis, Missouri.

A man walked past him, along the shore of the lake, making maladroit casts with a stubby fishing rod into the water at his feet. He wore only a bathing suit, pulled over his stomach in front; when he passed, carrying all that weight on the balls of his feet, matched arcs of pink flesh writhed over his kidneys with each step. It was Congressman John Olds, R. Mich. He waved without looking or interrupting the darting of the lure at his feet. "Nice to see you," Quinn called.

He sunned another hour, then started back through unlit woods to his house with its afternoon cap of light working its way across the front; by five it would slither off altogether and knot up in shadow at the north end, skate through the trees and disappear. Quinn thought about his conversation with Stanton and wondered how he could help him. Quinn was sentimental enough about their friendship as it had been. And though more had passed between them than he now cared to remember, their friendship seemed a necessary part of the future.

He heard a knocking at the door and went through the living room cautiously. He opened the door; it was Janey. She wanted Quinn to come over and try to console Stanton. He had been to see Olson and had come back despondent. He wouldn't say what had happened. Would Quinn please come?

Stanton was sitting up. He had a tray of food beside him and a pile of books on the end table. Tears were streaming down his face which was otherwise slack and drunken. Quinn knew he would be throwing himself into it; Stanton regarded himself, when drunk, as a third person for whom he was not responsible. The sky was the limit.

"You didn't mention the drinking," Quinn said to Janey in a clear conversational voice.

"Never mind that!" Stanton called. "You don't get off so easy!"

"What happened when you went to see Olson?"

"There was little fraternity or egality."

"Okay—"

"Rather, mistreatment."

"I'm going back."

"Don't! No fair—"

"This isn't fun for us, Vernor. We're all sober, you see."

"I pay a handsome price for my small pleasures," Stanton said slackly. "You can't come in here with your prayerbook—"

"All right, I don't have to—"

"May as well let him talk," Janey said.

"Let the spoilt priest talk," said Stanton. "Quinn, you've gone back on me. And Janey won't let me marry her. She won't do it. Commit any offense to nature. But simple Christian marriage? Not on your life."

"I would marry you if you were human," she said.

"Simple Christian marriage?" he asked. "Oh ho, no."

"Listen," Quinn started.

"Christian little ceremony?"

"Vernor—"

"Marriage?"

"Vernor—"

"Are you kidding? What? Her?" He clambered out from under the covers on all fours, wearing only his pajama top, his behind directed at the window. "God damn it, I want decent treatment around here! I want consideration and the rest of what was lost in the French Revolution! I want dreams, space, Listerine! I want . . . I want! GAAGH!" He flung himself over on his back, revealing a perfectly despicable and unwarranted erection; arms across his eyes, wallowing and blubbering spuriously. Janey backed away toward the door, wide-eyed. Suddenly she ran forward and began to hit Stanton on the chest. Stanton looked into the doorway at Quinn, his expression of hopeful surprise and wonder only occasionally flinching into a grimace. Finally, she stopped and went to the side of the room and slumped into a chair. "My!" said Stanton.

"I could have been a guide at the UN," said Janey, agonized. Quinn continued to stare at Stanton. Behind this devilish picture of Stanton many pictures receded into memory, bright and framed like the windows of a train. Without knowing what he was doing, Quinn resolved to act. He went to see Olson.

There was something not absolutely perpendicular about Olson. He slung himself in his doorway and his lower lip made an ample curve beneath his lengthy lower teeth. "Evening, Jack."

"What's . . . evening about it?"

"Yes, very good," Quinn said. Olson began patting his pockets in search of something he didn't find. "Have you and Stanton been talking?"

"Oh, hell, not really I wouldn't think. He rooted himself about half through my year's liquor supply—"

"Jack, you're stewed, aren't you?"

Olson danced about, shadow boxing. "Put up your dewks—!"

"Jack—"

"Put them up!"

"Jack—"

"Put them!"

"Have you and Vernor Stanton had a nice talk?"

"Put them up!" He danced a moment more and fell.

"Get up, Jack."

"I took a spill."

"I saw you did."

Olson dragged at Quinn's clothes getting to his feet. "What are you so interested for?"

"No reason." Quinn was extremely uncomfortable.

"I know they're getting rid of me, if that's what you mean. I know that—" He stopped. "But Stanton wasn't here about that, was he?"

"Well, yes, indirectly, he was."

"He was, ay. Sonofabitch. That clears your head. Is that what it was all about. I thought we was just going to tie one on." Quinn watched him shake off his inebriation. He walked up and down in front of his house with his hands on his head, looking now at Quinn and then into space with an immense question in his movements: he was overwhelmed and offended. "I'll be a sonofabitch," was all he could say. He looked over his shoulder at Quinn, amused and offended. "I've got to hand it to him. The bastard knows how to go after you. I've got to give him credit." Quinn left him. He would return when Olson's head had cleared and the information sunk in.

Look: Janey is packing on the first floor. Quinn stands and doesn't speak. From above, Stanton, up and shaving, sings "Fa, la, la!" with unique brutality. Quinn thinks, I must talk her out of it, she has nowhere to go, I have to make up for that swine. "Where are you going?"

"God, I don't know. Away."

"Where to?"

"Just away." She stands erect now in a sleeveless blue pullover and her arms are very slightly tanned. Quinn sees that she doesn't want to go and that now that he has begun to talk her out of it, she won't go. Still it is lamentable, Stanton rioting in his bed, yet served like a prince; and Janey down here with her bag on the floor and two or three pieces of clothing thrown in.

"Where will you go?"

She sat on the bag. "I don't know."

"What about Vernor?"

"I don't know, I don't know."

"Fa, la! Fa, la!" came the brutal voice. Stanton knew they were down here. Quinn wondered how he could let things get to such a sorry state. Worse, he suspected it was intentional. But to what end? To some end, that much was certain. Stanton was a deliberate man and knew how he got his effects. It used to be that behind all of his deliberate acts were abstract principles he could name, like courage, attainment, persistence; or irritation, interference, degradation. Quinn no longer knew how insistent Stanton was about this system; but he had a powerful suspicion that behind certain activities, the dueling or the episode on the bridge or at the Bug House, lingered these abstractions. The most unexpected of Stanton's deeds had always had such words behind them. Always before, when Quinn had been the victim, he had wondered helplessly what words Stanton linked with his aggressive efforts: antagonism? defeat? menace? And right now, he wondered what word hovered behind himself and behind Janey and what word linked Stanton to them; was it diversion? was it domination? was it revenge? Or none of these?

It was evening again. Quinn walked out onto his porch and sat down. The late sun, summery and vegetable, rotted in the trees before him. He felt that he had found something.

Janey removed the rubber band from the pack of photographs. She went through three or four and buried them in the deck before handing one to Quinn. It was of a middle-aged man standing as though on a wire between a small, defensive palmetto and an artesian well. "That is Daddy when he was in the mineral springs business. That well looks harmless enough but it smelled to high heaven. The water was used to manufacture a nutritious sodapop that induced vomiting every time. It was also used to make taffy and that wasn't so bad, although it changed the flavors a little. The cherry taffy tasted like bloodwurst. The lemon taffy tasted like chicken liver. Anyway, the mineral springs business?—it failed. Luckily, Daddy has a pension from the Civil Service and he has built a small house on the property. It is tremendously hot there and the only shade comes from that palmetto you see and there is the smell. There is that. Whenever I visit, the smell gets into my clothes and even my skin. But they use it for everything, cooking and washing included." She handed him another photo. It was of herself, younger, sitting in a crowd of seated people, young men all around her. The picture showed her the single still spot in a crowd of enthusiasts rising from, or falling back onto, bleachers. She was seated, fingers crisscrossed around the stems of wired carnations, abstracted. "Cotton Bowl, 1960." The next picture was a single shot of the palmetto followed by one of the artesian well, which had new poignancy for Quinn. Then the mother (Quinn by this time feeling privileged), as faceless as one of the thousands of mid-American roadside picnickers, stout, the backs of her arms full and long as thighs. Mother is standing before the Truman Memorial Library in Independence, Missouri, where she is fresh from failing to run into the former President browsing in the stacks. The next picture, snatched by Quinn, is of Janey sunbathing in a two-piece bathing suit in front of a monster vehicle that turns out to be a dune buggy. She is a goddess. Quinn's head shudders with recollection of his afternoon of sinistrality. In the background of the picture is the Gulf which, as it is out of focus, is overexposed in discs of whiteness; among them stand men in white crescents of overexposed foam: this is the S.M.U. outing on Padre Island, near Corpus Christi. The photographer is an All-Conference single-wing halfback. He can do poor imitations of Ferlin Husky and Johnny Cash but cannot play a musical instrument. Then Janey hands Quinn a picture probably taken from a rooftop; looking down, it shows the artesian well, center, and the palmetto, lower left; between the two is an indistinct expanse of naked, sandy soil; Quinn believes he sees the shadow of the photographer appended to the long triangle of the roof's shadow. Is it Janey? He doesn't ask.

Janey stopped selecting pictures from the pack and Quinn, with plenty to think about, didn't request another.

But he did ask if he could see more later and she answered that she carried a load of stuff with her in these little cases, everything from coral jewelry she bought in Puerto Rico to more pictures to lavaliers to catalogues of the Prado, the Pitti and the Uffizi galleries; and that he was welcome to look through it all; there was nothing she liked better than going through other people's belongings; nor Quinn, who intended in his gratitude to tell something about Stanton that would be admirable. He had intended so the minute he saw her today, but couldn't; not that there wasn't anything to tell, or that it wouldn't be understood. He didn't want to.

He went up to the club to call the office. He had neglected to check in and knew things would have piled up by now. The telephone was in the storage closet. On the shelf beside the phone there was a stack of old Pere Marquette directories which had grown in twenty years since the Second World War from nine to seventeen pages; and from five pages of Olsons to eleven. There was a chest of narrow, sectioned drawers, containing the flies that Jack Olson tied during the winter. The drawers were labeled with tape. Quinn pulled open the drawers and smelled the camphor. Inside each square section the flies were clustered new and perfect and infinitely more consequential-looking than the gross castings and fittings and flanges Quinn's factory produced. Next to the phone was a pencil sharpener with a rotating ring perforated with various-sized pencil holes, only one of which showed a graphite stain; on the floor below was a cone of fine shavings that Quinn for some reason wanted to put a match to and up would go flies, telephone directories, Centennial Club and Quinn of Quinn Industries. "Mary Beth?"

"Boss man!"

"Give me the news."

"I've got you booked solid as of July one."

"What's happening July one?"

"You're coming back . . ."

"How do you know?"

"Boss man!"

Business had windrowed nastily. Every sale or renewal marked a new all-time high. The factory picnic was coming up in two weeks, which affair marked the cycle of Quinn's business life: he had begun it by directing and producing the factory picnic of the year before. Mary Beth had taken the matter of customer gifts into her own hands and had subscribed to a service, run by canny New England sharpers, which shipped live lobsters at five times their real value in containers shaped like tricorn hats and decorated with facsimile signatures of the signers of the Declaration of Independence.

"I'll never come back," said Quinn, "you can't make me." He thought of the containers opened, dying lobsters crawling over his calling card.

Mary Beth had more surprises: he was now a charter subscriber to the Hamtramck Polish war memorial; he had bought twenty tickets to the Fourth of July Arc Welders' Ball; he had agreed to speak before the Dexter Jaycees; he had become a member of the Society of Production Consultants, whatever that was; his tax lawyer had made him chairman of the board instead of president, and so on. Quinn's interest flagged with these permutations and he grew wan. Mary Beth sensed his lassitude. She became assertive and seemed to swagger. Quinn was glad that they were separated by hundreds of miles of insulated wire. If he were in the office, she would make one of her outlandish bids for sex by hitching around the place in a way that aroused Quinn's scientific interest rather than his ardor.

Mary Beth was a Canadian and affected rugged Windsor tweeds that seemed to carry the stench of the highlands in them. She had pink cheeks too and sandy hair, genetically wind-tossed. Sometimes she brought Quinn presents from Ontario, cases of smuggled Moulson's ale or Cincinnati Cream or a small wheel of Black Diamond cheddar with a rind that cut away as cleanly as apple peel. This was a real service, unlike her secretarial work; and when Quinn saw the fine gold upright bottles of ale in his refrigerator next to the cloth-wrapped wheel of cheddar, he sometimes vowed to spread-eagle Mary Beth in the office and prong her devoutedly. But when he considered how he would get on with the day's work afterward, he reneged; because the vision of Mary Beth, rumpled and wearing a bonny, sated, pioneer grin was too bright on his mind. So he kept taking the cheese, the ale and, one fall, an oppressive, oily Indian sweater, thick and environmental; and Mary Beth remained doughty, vigorous, inefficient. She wrote "cheque" for "check" like an incorrigibly mandarin stylist and said "hoose," "roond" and "broon" for "house," "round" and "brown." Eventually, when she was sure that Quinn would be only considerate, she began to entertain callers,

99

salesmen, accountants, file clerks; at first a great many, most of them in blue serge suits, the kind of shoes issued for parade dress in the armed services, and discreet crew cuts of indeterminate color. Then a steady repeating few took Mary Beth out for long lunch hours from which she returned with the sated look Quinn had been obliged once to visualize for himself. Things got quiet and Quinn found he could go to his office and get his work done, though he sometimes met strangers in the hall or found condoms hovering in the toilet. He learned at last to live with it all.

Quinn left Mary Beth on the phone today with instructions to make a priority list of things he had to do and send it with appropriate files. He issued this directive precisely but with a sense of fighting back boredom. "Count on me," Mary Beth told him.

He had given Olson time to sober up. He walked to the small house to learn what had come of Stanton's visit. He cautioned himself against giving anything away if Stanton had said nothing. Olson's pride was a touchy and complicated matter. When he got there, he found the gate ajar and a cat slumbering in the yard and the Springer spaniel nowhere in sight. Then from the interior of the porch a man materialized in a white T-shirt, its right sleeve rolled around a pack of Lucky Strikes whose red spot showed as though staring. The man was heavy, maybe thirty-five.

"Is Jack in?"

"Jack is retired." The man came down the steps linking his fingers behind his head and thus revealing a bevel of flaccid belly.

"Retired? To where?"

"He mentioned Florida."

"Florida—"

"That's right."

"What'd he want to go to Florida for?"

"He heard about an opening for an alligator wrestler."

"*What?*"

"The man always wins. The alligator doesn't know they're wrestling. He allows himself to be tied in knots."

"I'm not interested in alligator wrestling as such. I—"

"All I can tell you is that he looked like he could wrestle alligators when he left. He was that mad."

"But you say Florida—"

"Oh, I don't know for sure. I'm taking a wild guess. I don't see anything *wrong* with Florida. Hot in the summer they say."

"Who are you?"

"What do you mean?" He was suspicious.

"What are you doing here?"

"I'm the new manager. My name is Earl Olive."

"Who hired you?"

"*Jack Olson!*"

Quinn stopped to take this in, swallowing it like a horse pill.

"What did you do before this?" Quinn asked.

"What do you want to know for?" The man leaned on the fence. His black hair was swept back on both sides and a few heavy strands fell down below his ears. The stretched T-shirt formed clean and square around the Luckies and the red spot now looked like a wound under the cloth. "Let me put it this way, I was in the live bait business."

"Like what kind of live bait?" Quinn asked; something quite intense had fallen over the conversation.

"Worms."

Quinn was conscious of the sound of the trees around them breathing in the wind.

"Worms? How did you get the worms?"

"Like everybody else," said the man after a pause. "I got the worms like everybody else. Okay?"

"I want something more specific than that."

"Look, you get a old crank telephone and cut off the phone part so all you got left is the box and crank. Then there is two wires and onto each one you hook a rod. Okay, you go out in a field and put the rods into the ground, right? And give the crank a turn, am I right? Then what happens?"

"Worms . . ."

"Worms pop out of the ground, big nightcrawlers, wrigglers, red worms, the whole bit. Now do you believe I was in the bait racket?"

"I never said I didn't believe . . . you."

"Listen to me: here is how you work the grasshoppers. First, build you a frame onto the front of an old car. Next, make you a cheesecloth net for the frame which is longer on the bottom than on the top. Then drive across a field with the whole apparatus at top speed. Do you follow? It can get dangerous. Check the net ever couple passes, are you with me? Sometimes there is a ton of hoppers. Now I see you are looking for the dangerous part: oncet I was collecting hoppers when the car lit into a enormous chuck hole and I pitched over the hood and buried myself in about four feet of them slimy hoppers. If I had of been knocked unconscious I would have smothered under them bugs. As it was, it near spoilt the live bait business for my part. —Now do you believe me?"

"Yes."

"See how it was dangerous and could of kilt me?"

"You bet I do, Earl."

"I handled frogs and frog harness, crickets, June bugs and hellgrammites. I was in the live bait business hand and foot. I had to cater to every live bait need. One fella would fish for bass with nothing but live baby mice. I had to have them. Another fella made a paste out of fireflies which he used to fish for brook trout. I had to have fireflies." He looked to Quinn as though for a long expected question.

Quinn didn't know what it might be but asked, uncertainly, "Where was this?"

"Boy you are full of queshtons. Okay, this was a few mile north of Ishpeming on the Yellow Dog river."

"Was that . . . a good location?"

"A bad location."

"What was wrong with it?"

"What was wrong with it? Nobody knew where I was at. How was they to know where I was at?"

"I don't know; but these people that wanted all these different baits . . ."

"Oh, God! They was steady customers! *That ain't a*

living!" Quinn, buffaloed, felt compelled to say he was sorry. Earl Olive took it in good grace.

"I was sorry too. I had a ton of live bait I couldn't sell and I had to fish it all myself. I fished the Yellow Dog, the Escanaba, the Ontanagon, the Two Heart, come down here and fished the Pigeon, the Black, the Au Train, the Jordan and the Pere Marquette where, guess who I met?"

Cautiously, "Who?"

"Jack Olson! I was fished out. I had fished bugs, frogs, hellgrammites, mice and worms. I hit the Jordan in the middle of the Caddis hatch and must have killed every trout in the river. I ran into your Jack Olson up to the tavern in Manton and told him all about it. I thought he fit to kill me. He said he hated any a man who would fish a trout with bait. I said it was all meat to me and he walked out the tavern. Next time I seen him was last night in the same tavern and he asked me did I want this job. Well, I had got so I couldn't look at a trout nor a piece of live bait; so I told him God damn right I wanted the job. *So,* then!" He went suddenly bashful. "Here I am!"

Representative John Olds, R. Mich., said: "Olson was a useful man. Which of us would deny that? But he was headstrong. He was hard to handle. He was a thorn in our sides. We are pleased to have him out of our hair. All this talk of property degenerating makes me tired. These woods and streams have a natural tendency to maintain themselves. We need a janitor and we've got one from the looks of this Olive. But whoever we have, our children and our children's children will frequent these lands *in perpetuam*. The traditions of the Centennial Club, thanks to its board of directors, will continue *de profundis*. I thank you."

"You're welcome."

"Yuh, okay."

Mrs. Enid "Cooky" Silt said: "A wise guy. Someone should have slapped his face. I'm glad he's gone." Impossible, thought Quinn, could Olson have seduced Mrs. Silt? Very hard to imagine; one thought he had better taste. Quinn was frankly appalled at the thought of those Mamie Eisenhower bangs damp with lascivious sweat, the fly-tying hands of that admirable woodsman busy.

Old Mrs. Newcombe and her husband agreed that times change, off with the old, on with the new. It is written that history is no respecter of persons.

Quinn found Spengler, the chronicler of the Centennial Club, below the spillway of the dam that regulated the level of the lake and kept its constant shoreline. He was sketching the punks that grew in the backwater there. Beside him was a pair of binoculars. He was on the lookout for Kirtland's warbler which lived only in this county and wintered on Abaco island in the Bahamas. The chronicle was to come out on the Fourth of July, the centennial celebration of the club's founding.

The chronicle would contain an account of punks, of Kirtland's warbler and of Olson. He wasn't talking till then.

Scott said: "Our ideas of declining fortunes have changed since the seventeenth century. In the Low Countries, Huizinga argued—" He went on, too.

Stanton said: "I'm not qualified to answer, old sport. Unfortunately, Olson has become a non-person for me. He never was. So, how can I tell you whether or not I'm glad he's gone." Then he grinned. "Isn't the new guy god-awful?"

Two nights later, the shooting began, waking everyone. Five shots rang out in the muggy night from behind the lake. Stanton appeared at Quinn's in the morning. Quinn dressed and they hiked around the back side of the lake, breaking through the swale and basswood tangle. Presently, they came upon a place where the cover had been battered down and trampled. In the middle were a grown doe and a very young buck of fifty or sixty pounds. Whoever had shot them had started to hog-butcher the doe but had got nervous and ripped loins off the two quickly and beat it. So the little buck was nearly whole; while the doe was vented up to the sternum with the glossy spillage of intestines and jellying blood. Since neither animal had been bled, it would be certain that even the meat was spoiled.

Quinn ate dinner at the lodge. He scribbled drafts

of business letters beside his plate and when he was finishing the meal, Janey came in and sat opposite him and said, "There you are." She had caught him unexpectedly and for a moment they conversed very unnaturally. He called for coffee and she put on her dark glasses, doubtless from the same embarrassment; and they cut off her softening eyes so that her nose and cheeks were clear beveling lines around the glasses. Quinn reached across and removed them. He said he hadn't meant to make her nervous. He folded the glasses and pushed the dishes to one side. Janey undid the rubber band from a fresh pack of pictures. "You wanted more," she declared.

"And I do."

"Then get the expression off your face. Sometimes my memory fails and I use these to prove I was around last week. Here, let's do it this way. You ask for a particular kind of picture."

"How do you mean?" Quinn asked and she glanced at the pack.

"Okay, for example, ask me for a ridiculous picture."

"Right. Give me a ridiculous picture."

She handed him Stanton's Harvard graduation picture.

"Now you think of one," she said.

"A sad picture."

"A sad picture," she repeated as she went through the pack. "A sad picture." She looked up. "Well, it turns out . . . they're all sad."

"Then give me them all." She handed him the pack. "Why did you come over here tonight?"

"Because Vernor is giving me a very hard time."

"What for?"

"Just for drill, he said."

"All right, let's never mind him and look at pictures. Who's this?" It was her cousin Richard, a rock and roll singer who was killed in a plane crash. He came from a branch of the family that was out of favor for having struck oil enough for them all in East Texas and dissipating the fortune; because of this, Janey said, she herself had been taught all the little economies, a thousand useless tools to be used in the face of squandered fortunes. She said that this ruined branch was the family's most interesting. It had taken its chances and burned hotly for a few years in the thirties when everybody else was lost in the dust bowl. They had thrown up an impressive mansion outside Orange, Texas, that, even though it belonged to them no more, was still there. They had owned three celebrated race horses: Steamboat, Shanty Duchess and Dogdancer who killed his trainer. True, nothing had worked out: the boy dead, the father, summoned for managerial malfeasance, was jailed for fraud. The mother, a poor farm girl at twenty, just as poor at sixty, affected antiquated French lace getups that showed the delicate tanning of the flatiron at home, an unmistakable, though mistaken, impression of down-at-the-heels gentility; she got the modicum of gallantry unaccorded the less romantic poor in the South.

The next picture is of the palmetto, the mother, the father, the artesian well; you still cannot see the house though its shadow has moved farther toward the well and sweeps past the couple who are old enough now that they must have been living in the house some time.

The palmetto is larger, miraculously retaining the exact shape of its youth. Though the picture must have been taken ten years after the visit to Independence, Missouri, Quinn imagines that he sees in her face her failure to encounter the former President in his memorial library.

"Are these people still alive?"

"Pretty much."

Janey sighed and looked out the window. The sun was clear and late and hurtled through the trees, lighting a soup of pollen that thickened gold. It seemed a long way from Texas, a long way from the drill-master nearby who strained under his jokes in this same forest.

Business: the time had come to plan the factory picnic. The very thought threw him back, not unhappily, upon his origins as a man of affairs. His first job after taking over had been to organize the factory picnic. And to have so soon to plan it again gave him an exceedingly unpleasant sense of *déjà vu*. The first time, he had worked carefully, interviewing employees to determine what was wanted. Since the company employed many of the handicapped, the mainstays were out: three-legged races, leapfrog and so on. The emphasis therefore would have to be a sedentary one, and Quinn arranged for the delivery of truckloads of keg beer, and epic quantities of fried food. There would be Bingo with a professional caller and personalized (initialed) Bingo tokens; the prizes were chosen by what was considered uncanny judgment: glasspack "Hollywood" mufflers for cars, white rubber mudflaps with safety reflectors, turkeys, porkpie hats, barbecue sets, pink concrete yard flamingos, TV trays, plastic dogs that sat in the rear window of your car and wobbled their heads, plastic lions that sat in the rear window of your car and winked right or left when you used your turn signal, Mohawk bow-and-arrow sets, Chief Pontiac headdresses, risqué place mats, glass shower doors with leaping stags sandblasted onto their surfaces, and many other odds and ends related to automobiles, television, child diversion and sexual insinuation. The band presented a special problem because it had to be able to play both country music and polkas or it would not satisfy. Quinn had to do the auditioning and, here again, it was something of a mudbath of expanding and contracting accordions, broad Middle European faces and long, sidehill Anglo-Saxon, the electric guitars that were played in front of you with one hand plucking and the other manipulating an iron bar that sent undulant notes into the room like sea serpents; occasionally there would be a female lead singer in lacquered beehive hair whose batlike cries aroused Quinn's interest; he would consider for a moment then, like some arbitrary crank, say that he would have to insist on polkas. Finally, as if desire had been made flesh, a quartet from River Rouge materialized in his offices, set up their equipment and with mechanical regularity played first a polka and then a country song. Nonstop. So Quinn had a band; he had prizes, activities, and he rented a small fairground with a copse of knobby, pollard elms and a brown duck pond.

Now for the picnic: the picnic did go well up to the last minutes; and the drinking had already reached a merry peak; but the minute prizes ran out, something saturnalian set in and the fighting began; the band played only when threatened; Quinn pulled grunting, punching men apart; doctored a woman who had got a heavy blow from behind. Once an enormous punch press operator began to lay about him violently with a frozen turkey, sending people screaming toward the duck pond. Quinn, trying his best to keep out of it, had to threaten firing to disarm him and the man went behind the Bingo pavilion and wept like a woman. Gradually, it began to grow calm though; and the most marked sound soon became the chatter of the old ladies at the beer counter. They had heretofore been unable to get to the head of the line; now the beer was almost gone and the great, dull silver kegs wheezed foam and moaned like barrel organs. At that moment, the finale began.

A green Chevy sedan with no one at the wheel came gliding at moderate speed, sending people running and dragging children out from in front of it. It came, stately and carnauba-waxed, pristine with its bullnose, customized hood, bubble skirts, blue-tinted windows, jiggling kewpie in the empty, azure interior, and Augustan rumble of dual exhausts; curved slowly and miraculously away from the duck pond and cracked to a stop against a pollard elm. Now everyone ran. Quinn ran, toward the car nuzzling the tree, its hind wheels churning the grassless fairground soil behind. Quinn pulled open the front door of the car to turn off the ignition and his janitor rolled out blue and vein-laced in a diabetic coma, a tiny, distant scream coming from somewhere behind the locked strenuous jaws, the chest seizing under the printed Miami palms of his sportshirt. Someone pushed in beside Quinn, authoritatively worked upon the jaws until

they opened and shoved in the end of a Pepsi-Cola bottle, glass clinking against teeth, and began to pour as his
other hand worked the janitor's tongue free. For the
others, this was simply the last straw and they began
to leave. Quinn, kneeling beside the janitor, watched his
eyes come out of their knotting as the Pepsi spilled
around his neck and into the holiday shirt, watched the
eyes grow clear and apologetic as he saw the retreat.

But Monday, when everyone was back docilely at the
machines, Quinn was amazed to find that the party had
been a success. "A good time was had by all," his foreman confided. And behind Quinn's grateful smile was a
vision of brawling men, of their elderly mothers and
mothers-in-law with somber, ill-concealed cases of beer
farts, and the children themselves, all gullet, fighting
over prizes and destroying everything in their paths like
army ants. Still, Quinn's smile was grateful and it was
genuine.

Nevertheless, moving along the production line, which
was lubricated to near silence, brought him the sense
that these useful, efficient men were right now at their
most minatory. The workers placed and removed, placed
and removed before the presses, rhythmically; they bowed
to the machine, propitiating it with a piece of cold rolled
steel or a bright, solar aluminum disc; and the machine
returned the bow and returned the gift, now miraculously
transformed into something of purest utility. Moments
later, these same objects appeared on the other side of
the factory, hung on hooks, like ex-votos, and they glided
through a bath of neoprene and into the ultraviolet dry-

ing rooms. The next day, out the door they went to their numberless destinies.

Yet, re-creating it in his mind, the old party held no lesson for the new; and Quinn saw no way of improving. Clearly, however, while there had been prizes, the fighting was at a minimum; that was a detail: more prizes. If only he could do it all by remote control, program the entire picnic on a punch card and keep himself far, far from their joys. He would wear a black silk tuxedo, a boiled linen shirt whiter than Antarctica, and on their day give them the occasional kindly thought.

He went to the lake to sit on the cutter. Summer was here and there was a portable lifeguard tower with a golden Teuton aloft. Quinn began immediately to run into acquaintances. He met Sheila Derndorff, a pretty girl of twenty with merry teeth, who had broken both legs dancing. Then he met, directly under the lifeguard tower, undulant in flaglike madras, Charles Murray, a gifted trial lawyer from Cincinnati and amateur of literature who had, fifteen years before, in an extravagant gesture of literary Anglo-faggotry, become a Roman Catholic. To have been born a Catholic and lapsed, as Quinn had done, was intolerable to Murray who nevertheless continued to regard Quinn as an accomplice in the international Romish plot. Today, he began by lamenting anew the passing of Pius Twelve, the last, in his view, of the intransigent aristocratical Popes, whose death began an age of unparalleled prole boobery in Rome. He meant, naturally, Pope John, whom he called a "loutish mountain wop." Yes, Quinn agreed, yes, yes, yes. Murray's left hand was clutched around a pair of tortoise-shell sunglasses. He wore a raw-silk summer blazer and squinted conspiratorially at the sun. Behind him a fat woman herded children, her pocked buttocks lurching with the effort. "Your friend Stanton is going to start a squabble around here," Murray confided. "And I am anxious to see—*Hi, Janet darling! You better run! Or I'll bite your leg!*—to see how it turns out."

"I am too."

"Look, will you excuse me?"

"Of course." Murray didn't hear. He was chasing Janet, a great-thighed girl in pedal pushers. She ran enticingly from Murray who pursued, holding both hands in the air, one retaining the cigarette, the other the tortoise-shell glasses. Janet wasn't making cases. And Quinn suspicioned Murray thought of orthodox domestic arrangements, sensibly made. It happened that Janet, Fortescue's sole heir, was a highly successful engineer. Quinn entertained himself with visions of the arrangement, Murray advancing, Janet retreating; Janet advancing, Murray retreating; and before his eyes they did so, cutting and swerving in the dark lake sand, the still lake behind in the hot sun, throwing its single, wobbling flash of light. The golden lummox on the lifeguard tower gazed pitiless and hieratic upon the crescent of sunbathers with their towels and oils and paperback books. Across the lake, in deep bays of shadow, a canoe floated without movement. A fisherman cast peacefully with a rod that was a shiny filament at that distance. As Quinn walked along, the mothers rose up from towels, oiled and gleaming like seals, and glared into the sky before letting down again. Quinn browsed, hands behind, checking out the younger women, imagining giving them the old one-two; remembered newspaper accounts of infidelity among young marrieds and love rackets in the suburbs; why not shocking sex bash at exclusive trout club? One young woman lay before him, between him and the Teuton; she was even more golden than the latter with long brown legs and well-shaped feet; she lay upon her stomach, her face turned to one side, apparently asleep; the opening of her pretty mouth in that incandescently sunlit face seemed to Quinn the blackest stripe of pure void; and he stared at her until it made her sit up, return his look with hot distraction, and pour sun lotion down her cleavage; the oil emerged from under the bra of the bathing suit and sought her navel in slim, golden progress. Beside her was the child, an imperious infant who beat the sand with the flat of a little shovel and said, "Garbo! Garbo!" Quinn was embarrassed by her gaze. He snapped his fingers, consulted his watch, started off purposefully and fell. He pushed his hands through the sand as though sampling its warmth, hummed as if satisfied and, with beating face, looked over at the mother. Now she looked straight into him. The sun upon her and upon the infant ignited them savagely, and the lifeguard never moved. The woman's eyes followed him, hung on him, as he got to his feet. He stood a moment, then went off. When he looked back, mother and child were as still as graven images and, like the lifeguard, didn't move. Quinn made his way, his retreat, up the path, glancing back at the woman, the others too on the dark sand or wading in the lake's sun-lit, transparent margin.

Quinn thought: The hell with these unreckonable quantities. I'm a businessman. Besides, the lake was for women and children. If you didn't want to shoot, drink or fish you were to have joined the Y. He went to the lodge, called the factory and talked to his manager. The manager assured him that things weren't completely out of control but that they were tough, that's all, tough. Material shortages were slowing production. This was Quinn's clue. Material shortages in this case were always unnecessary, and Quinn saw that this trip was a mistake. This lapse was going to mean an inexcusable loss of orders. He saw now that the resonance and responsive-ness of the company to his ministrations was matched by a mirror-image potential for decline. He couldn't set it up and let it run as he had planned. It was like a bicycle and when he stopped pedaling, it stopped.

In his mind's eye, a character that looked like Blind Pew was nailing up a sign that read BANKRUPT. By turns, Quinn holds his hammer for him, the sign, the nails, grows voluble and offers to buy him a drink.

Stanton was wearing the linen shorts of the first day.
"Been practicing in the gallery?" Quinn asked.
"Count on it. Air heavy with eventualities. Gin and tonic?"
"Just tonic would be fine. Hello, Janey."
"Hello."
"How are you . . ."

"She's fine. Why no gin? Here." He gave him the drink.
"It spoils the essential purity of the tonic."
"That so."

The porch was made like the room of a ship. The screened panels were held in place by half-round strips and brass screws; the strips had been imprecisely painted and the pores of the screen were filled for an uneven inch or so around their perimeters. Overhead, narrow varnished rafters divided the roof into regular strips of coarser wood. And above the screen were rolled canvas awnings. Quinn sat in one Hong Kong wicker chair, Janey in another; her arm hung in repose; her forefinger rested on the floor. Stanton strode on reliable, earth-gripper feet with their high tan arches and said, "Do you know, I didn't fire Olson?" Quinn sensed a prepared question and tried to dodge it.

"What's the new fellow's name?"

"Earl something or something Earl. I forget. But I didn't fire Olson and I didn't hire what's his name."

"I talked to this guy actually. He used to be in the bait business—"

"I want to set the record straight about Olson—"

"—live bait."

"The older members got hot around the collar and figured Olson had to go. And I didn't like the sight of those two little deer. That also is for the record."

"Don't be coy. You made a move that was just extra stupid. Your speech the night we fished—it finished Olson."

"James, you seem to have a backlog of bad feeling going for you—"

117

"You played up to the kind of stupidity we always hated, which is unedifying enough. But then this cutesie stuff after—" Stanton had to cut in.

"Be firm with me, father, I have sinned. My last confession was invalid."

The new manager was at the door.

"We're talking about you. What's your name?"

"Earl Olive." Olive came in and looked the place over like a demolitionist. He was wearing flamboyant cowboy clothes. "Just a couple questions," he said, eyes sweeping over and around everything, including Janey, but seeing nothing to boost, settling on Stanton. "What do you know about these two deer?"

"Both dead."

"Notice anything unusual?"

"Only you, Earl."

"Have any clues? Or suspicions?" Earl pushed his Stetson back on his head with one finger under its frontmost edge.

"Yeah," said Stanton, "Jack Olson or friends of Jack Olson."

"He has an alibi," said Olive.

"In the nature of what?"

"In the nature of drunk as a skunk," Olive said. Quinn saw that this conversation was pleasant to Stanton in its contentiousness. "You know, Earl," Stanton said, "Jack Olson was a real manager. He was a champ in his own way. Now around here the word is that you're no more than a janitor."

"You don't say."

"Well, don't you have any feelings about that?"

"My only feelings is that these folks't say I'm no more than a janitor might find themselves settling for a sight worse than that." This was nearly the last thing he said. He was having a barbecue to celebrate his new job and had to be off. A few minutes after he left, Quinn was wondering about this barbecue and so were Stanton and Janey.

In the beginning, they watched from a distance. Earl Olive had a washtub full of coals on a metal stand and he stood before it in a huge white puff of a chef's hat, turning meat. His friends sat on the stoop of his porch or swigged quart bottles of beer with their girl friends. One tanned and heavily lined man in an azure shirt that let you see through to his sleeveless undershirt and whose hair was as black as cinders and curled up into a sculptural pompadour, trapped a fat lady between a tree and his desperately pumping pelvis while Earl Olive, without watching him, yelled, "What the hell, Lucy? What the hell?" In front of the low fence that Olson had made were the cars and a few Harley-Davidson motorcycles with automobile-size tires, enormous saddles shaped like sections of a pie and more chrome fixtures than a motel bathroom. Earl Olive forked a piece of the cooking meat and held it out toward the trees, what looked like just trees, and said, "You wont some? Come own, you hungry? Say so and Earl Olive will feed you." Beyond the party and before the trees, others could be discriminated in the shadows. This group included Fortescue, Krauss, Edith Terrell, Jensen, Van Duzen, Murdock, Spengler, Laidlaw and Scott. This was a different group from Earl

Olive's; for one thing, it was quieter and showed more solidarity; and they stood in dense, composite order, reminding Quinn of opening a can of sardines and finding, from left to right, a row of heads, a row of triangles, a row of diamonds, and a row of tails: unity. In contradistinction, Earl Olive's group was disunited. Some were drinking, some talking, some trying to breed. Also, they were quite loud while the club group was very quiet. And they moved more; it was pointed out, for example, that at least one chap, the one in the see-through shirt, had a woman against a tree and was making a recognizably filthy motion against her. In fact, this same fellow yelled to Earl Olive that he was going to "do" her. The others in Earl's group made a good deal of inchoate noise and Earl himself occasionally spoke directly to the club group, offering food, beer, or asking rhetorical questions. On the other hand, the group from the club said not one thing.

Earl Olive's group seemed to have fun. The Centennial Club seemed to have none at all. Between the two there was something like a magnetic field. Two horseshoes faced each other and in between were many wavy lines. Perhaps it wasn't a magnetic field between the two groups. But there was a strong sensation of these wavy lines.

Then Fortescue stepped forward, forthright in his twills, and called, "Earl?" Quinn wondered who would get Fortescue's tin soldiers when he died.

"Howdy."

"What about keeping the noise down?"

"Let's keep the noise down!"

"And, oh, Earl—"

"Can I help you?"

"This other business—" He indicated the couple at the trees. "We've got ladies here." Fortescue turned an open hand behind him to draw attention to the club's womenfolk, lined behind Fortesque like a cabinet of fire-axes in an institutional boiler room. The man in the see-through shirt stepped up his activity and was now a veritable dervish at the tree.

"Bobby, best cut it out. You're making these folks horny."

"What you got's better," the man called, gone quite mad in his threshing.

"Earl!" Fortescue's reproach was no longer a secret.

"Caint stop, Earl! Caint stop!"

"Lucy!" Earl Olive called, pointing with a meat fork. "Can't you make an escape?" He turned to Fortescue's group. "He has been happy cuffin it for some many years we had no idea this could happen—" Scott took the lead.

"All right, kids," he said to the club group. "This is a little rank. Desmond? Edith? Let's go. Maureen, Janet? A little rank. Let's go, kids. I'll handle this."

"Winkin?" said Earl Olive. "Blinkin, let's go. Nod, are you coming?"

"I will want to talk to you," said Fortescue.

"You are talking to me," Olive said complacently.

Then Charles Murray, the Cincinnati lawyer, disengaged himself from the retreat and came back to the ring, and his short rapid stride seemed determined. He stepped before Earl Olive and, with his feet close together, rose slightly on his toes, at the same time holding up the folded tortoise-shell glasses as though they were a writing instrument and he were going to make a single, clear mark on a sheet of paper. "You," he said, "shall feel the full weight of my displeasure. I will remember this." Earl Olive looked at him, delighted.

"Okay, Heidi," he said, "you do that." Quinn tried to comprehend how it was that Charles Murray went away; but it wasn't quite like anything he had ever seen before. Without turning from Earl Olive, all of him seemed to rise in a low rearward arc, rising on his toes, retreating hands rising too as though they would sustain him in some low batward menace of going off. He was only walking away.

"Gee," said Janey, "that looks bad."

At his rare best, Stanton had the uncomplicated goodness of those who can talk to strangers. One knew that at his worst he was a joker and, to that extent, demonic. But at his best he had a simplicity that was not Quinn's and that Quinn envied, an ability to walk into the middle that Quinn, the calculator, lacked.

So Stanton led and Quinn followed with Janey on his arm. Stanton introduced himself all around, smoothly overriding country reticences, and then introduced Quinn and Janey to each of them flawlessly. He began, after that, to quip with Earl Olive as though from acquaintanceship immemorial.

"Where's my dinner, Earl?"

"Shit."

"What you done with my God damn dinner?"

"Sheeyit." Earl looked over his shoulder from the fire.

"Bobby, these folks wont some fuckin beer." Bobby brought three cold Pabst Blue Ribbon beers.

"Thank you," said Janey in a high voice. Now the others approached the fire warily. One girl stared at the side of Quinn's face until he looked over; and her smile which had been halfway up went all the way up. "Hi."

"Hi." Quinn swigged back half his Pabst Blue Ribbon. He hadn't been introduced to this girl. Now Earl was smiling at him.

"Good, huh?"

"You bet," said Quinn, smacking his lips just like in the advertisement: Say! That's good! And! It doesn't fill me up!

"Gimme a sip," said the girl, her yummies making rather a good thing of her short-sleeved pink sweater. Quinn gave her the can. She tilted it to her mouth a moment and handed it back. It was empty.

"All kidding aside," Stanton was saying, "we already ate, Earl. You just go on and make pigs of yourselves. We don't mind." Earl's arms fell to his sides, his chin to his chest; he commenced to jiggle all over.

"You tickle me," he managed, "I swear you do!"

"Jim," Quinn answered. "Jim Quinn. What's yours?"

"Lu."

"Hi, Lu."

"Hi."

Lu had a short little skirt of aniline blue that exposed the dimply legs. She wore low, fur-lined après-ski boots that Quinn ignored: the ski shops introduced a misunderstood element into the North.

The sun going off took the color out of Earl Olive's fire and it burned pale as frost under the skewered meat. Earl had one hand plunged far into his pocket while the other delicately rotated the skewer. Stanton told him the only way he'd eat anything he cooked was if it was drowned in ketchup and if he could chase it with a quick fifth of Pepto-Bismol so it wouldn't repeat on him. Earl Olive heaved all over and said my God you tickle me, oh Jesus.

"So what is it you do anyway?" Lu asked.

"I make parts for cars."

"Like what kind of parts for cars."

"Triangular ones with holes in them."

"Yeah? Wow. Is it hard?"

"Not at the moment."

"You guys sure," Earl called, "that you don't want any meat?"

"Positive."

Janey came up. "Would you get me a beer?" she whispered. "Vernor drank mine."

"What? Oh, sure. Here—" Quinn went to an open cardboard box and fished out two more Pabst Blue Ribbons.

Bobby stepped over, a beer in his hand curled up close to his chest. "Lemme crack them bastards for you." He had an opener on a long silvery cable attached to one of his belt loops. He opened the two beers and gave them to Quinn. Quinn thanked him and handed one to Janey.

"Thank you," she whispered, made one slice of her eyes toward Lu and rejoined Stanton. Quinn thought: what does she see? What does Janey see?

Meanwhile, Bobby and the fat girl got on the Harley-

Davidson and began driving through trees and brush. Lu explained that this was called "gardening," tearing up the earth, a sport developed during the war by teenagers who specialized in the highspeed wiping out of victory gardens by the skillful use of the power slide. Quinn nodded, listening first to her and then to the snarl of the motorcycle working its way up and down the hill through the ferns herbivorously, making purposeful back-and-forth casts so that when it wasn't on top of the hill and quite dark against the sky, it was below and all that was visible were the twin ovals of flame at its tailpipes. Still, above the rude exhaust came the fat girl's wild, loony cackle. Stanton came over. "How do you like that?" he asked. The motorcycle was now swiveling and skidding up the hill toward them.

"I guess I don't."

"What! Where is your sense of history? The bumpkin is motorized. It could have been exactly the same in the beloved Middle Ages where everything begins, dueling, everything. Look: you still have the peasant in his leather jerkin. Only now he's on a motorcycle instead of his wife's ass—" Janey looked up at him and he didn't return her glance.

"Hey!" said Lu. "There's ladies present!" She smiled at Janey and Janey smiled back with delicate strain. Quinn opened another beer.

"Piggy," said Stanton, "I've watched you."

"I've watched you," Quinn said, "through an unrewarding month."

"Come own," said Earl, joining them. "Eat something!"

"I couldn't possibly, Earl," Stanton said. Earl had a

substantial gobbet on the end of his cooking fork. He looked upon Stanton with devotion. "I have to watch Quinn and see that he doesn't get artificially elated." Lu giggled and pushed her baby fingers into Quinn's ribs. Stanton looked at her and Janey turned away.

Five minutes later, when the sound of the motorcycle had stopped without the machine's reappearing, Quinn tilted the can up precisely so that the acrid beer ran thinly over his teeth. He could see Lu over the arc of the can. He tried: "You want to see if we can find Bobby and the other one?" One of those timed silences that try the heart followed.

"Okay."

The spoor of the Harley was clear down the face of the hill; feather-shaped blades of earth turned up, smashed twigs and ferns down to a broad skid mark in soft ground and a place where the rear wheel had dug in half a foot and the exhaust had scorched and withered the foliage behind. Lu made downhill use of Quinn's arm and when he kissed her hotly she ran her hands up and down him in three-foot swipes saying, "Darling!" But when he tried to delay she insisted they press on. Quinn wasn't interested. So Lu took the lead, scouting forward into the brush ahead where the trail was still clear, bulled and busted through the tag alders downward. Now the light was quite diminished because the trees behind were west of them. The trail leveled into dried-out lowlands and a meadow of dead cattails waving stiffly in the slight wind. It looked as if the motorcycle would have been easy to manage here; the soil was flat and the cattails easy to batter down. But as though from violent impatience, the skid marks had become reckless, prolific and the cattails were slashed and battered in every direction. Twenty feet along this trail and they began hearing voices. Lu going ahead waved for silence from the already silent Quinn. He closed in alongside her and they went along Indian fashion, choosing their footing among the dry and broken stalks. In a moment, the twilight glinting of the huge motorcycle was visible through the vegetation and there was the smell of leaking gasoline harsh and unnatural in the decay of the lowland, the smell of which was sweet as yeast. Five more feet brought them the scene: the motorcycle slouched in chromium enormity, its wedge of finned cylinder heads in a calligraphy of shadow, exhausts sweeping back to the goiter bulge of mufflers and stopping at clean, beveled ends. On the great seat the fat girl knelt, naked, and holding the handlebars. Her throat was a curving arch, her face which was that of a sympathetic Irish policeman, implored the sky in silence. Her breasts were small but her stomach, full and pendant, hung toward the mirroring fuel tank of the machine. Bobby stood to one side of the clearing, also naked, smoking a cigarette and squinting in thought, holding the cigarette up close in front of his face. Presently, he stooped and rubbed it out, walked to the motorcycle and crouching on its footpegs behind her, sexually assaulted his companion who managed to keep her balance holding on only one-handed while the other hand was plunged deep into her full head of hair. She nickered.

"*Now!*" said Bobby, and she swung down one enormous leg adroitly, thrust the kickstarter and, as the machine roared, swung the leg back to kneel on the seat and, letting the engine return to idle calmly, crooned into the treetops.

"*Now razz the pipes!*" The fat girl twisted the throttle, the engine raged and Bobby's bony frame flailed in an uncanny hucklebuck. "*Now first gear!*" She moved a lever, crooning. Bobby flailed. "*Now pop the clutch!*" Two great tulips of flame expanded suddenly and the motorcycle lurched into the brush with its strange burden, roared maniacally and died, presumably crashed or fallen over. Quinn hadn't the heart to follow. Lu was sitting on the ground rocking back and forth and moaning. Quinn intuited that the performance had not been inspirational for her; and, perhaps, that was it: *no kisses!* The redeeming thing to do, he thought, would be to give her a small, fond, almost sibling, kiss. He did so and her jaw seemed to fall open a foot. Lu's little dimpled hand was in his fly, jerking his private adroitly until it was revealed and mouthed swiftly as an hors d'oeuvre. A moment later her outer garments were in a pile and the plump little highschooler sat in real stag magazine underwear, French thrust bra and net panties with sewed-on dominoes. Then, even these were gone too. She had small, smeared breasts and, legs apart, slight ridges of flesh gathered at her hips. She hauled Quinn in, already drawing and counterthrusting with a learned voracity that caused in the confused young businessman an orgasm he thought would roll his spine like a cloth window shade. Afterward, when he sat staring, he saw Lu behind a low bush ten feet away. Only her face showed smiling sleepily; he heard a delicate whiz in the leaves. When she came back he watched her dress.

"Jimmy," she said, bending over insanely and feeling the ground for something misplaced, "I have something to tell you."

"You weren't a virgin," Quinn said.

She stood up. "Why did you know that? You can't always tell that."

"I was just talking," Quinn said in the same stunned voice.

"My mother always told me to sit tight until Mr. Right popped the question."

"I sure didn't pop any questions." Quinn laughed.

"Who said you were Mr. Right?" Lu tied the angora collar around her neck. She gave Quinn a little hug and said "Darling!" peremptorily. They headed for the barbecue again.

"James," Stanton said, "you be second."

"What for?" Bobby and the fat girl were eating grilled meat with lazy stupefied movements, both sitting on the motorcycle. Quinn wondered how they beat him back.

"Earl here called me a raunchy mother and I had to challenge him to a duel."

"I'm ready to roll!" said Earl Olive. "Come own."

"Don't fall for it," Quinn told Earl. "I've been shot in the face, in the chest, in the throat. He never loses."

"He'll lose this time."

"No he won't. I promise you."

"I have handled virtually every type of pistols. Come own."

He started off, Stanton skipping beside him. Quinn followed. Janey passed him and joined Stanton, glancing back reproachfully at Quinn who wondered if it was for not having been more effective against Stanton. Then suddenly Lu took his hand in her baby fingers. She looked up with yearning and said, "Before, I was down in the dumps. Now I feel real excellent."

"That makes *me* feel good," Quinn said. She pressed her face to his arm a moment.

"Know what else? You're cute. Know that? You're cute as a bug!"

Quinn watched the loading of the guns, a pair of drab English horse pistols of the eighteenth century. When Stanton said that the wax bullets were only to indicate the winner, Quinn went into details; and when Stanton poured double charges Quinn argued. Olive was not impressed. Quinn warned Olive to protect himself and then began the counting. At ten, Earl Olive whirled into a gunfighter's posture, feet wide apart, crablike, left arm crooked out parallel to the ground, the gun low and forward and the face thrust toward the elegant Stanton in fatal invitation. He fired just an instant before Stanton who, Quinn now well knew, held his fire. Stanton, left hand on his hip, was untouched; he then shot and connected with Earl Olive who screamed and whirled, holding his face. The pistol slipped from between his hands and fell onto the floor spinning. Earl's hand came down from his face. His nose was broad and bleeding. He began to stalk Stanton who, without looking at him, carefully hung the horse pistol in the cabinet, turned back as Earl Olive swung wide, missing him, lunged and missed again as Stanton danced away. When Earl Olive recovered himself, Stanton jabbed out flat, leaning very slightly forward at the waist, the right hand crimped up close, and centered Earl Olive's face with a terrible sound. Olive groaned and swung wildly. Stanton stepped into the blow, taking it on the shoulder in order to swing deeply and heavily into Earl's stomach so that he went right down onto the hard floor, his wind knocked out, making his lungs rake to regain it. Earl Olive lay in complete physical defeat, the side of his face pressed against the floor, his knees drawn up, his hair splashed out from his still head. Quinn's ears rang and he went to the stairs. He looked back at Vernor's wondering face, his hands plunged deep in his pockets. He felt then that Stanton was only bad.

He sat down upstairs and lit a cigarette. He looked around the empty living room and gnawed at his lip. An instant later, Earl Olive crashed the door open as he went out, making a strained, humming noise that broke as soon as he was invisible in the darkness to a harsh reiterated howl of animal rage. Quinn sat straight upright; even his nervousness was gone; everything but his attention was gone, until the howling stopped. When that happened, his composure left him and he started gnawing the lip again.

Stanton came up. He looked into the darkness where Olive had gone. "I hardly know what to say," he said, his tongue lingering on the consonants as though he was about to stutter. "The scene seems to have had its origins in the epics of the Wild West. I never, *never* imagined . . . That nice bait purveyor and *likable* peasant. But no, shooting at me and hunting me is not to be allowed. M-my position here is well, *essentially* that of

the nobleman." Quinn groaned. Stanton went on, avert-
ing his face. "In any event, I pay bills here. I do not,
repeat, do not collect a salary and will not be patronized
or stalked by those who do." He stopped and reflected.
"Let's look at the good side. Let's notice how this polar-
izes things. Olive's dealings with me and the other members make him the enemy within. May I predict that
this is not going to be the usual boring, phlegmatic summer? May I predict that it is going to be a little more
. . . athletic? I have to make this place livable and the
old low-key razzmatazz just doesn't do it. When I arrived
I did everything I could to make things interesting. I
told jokes. I did imitations. I wore funny hats—I had
one with windows, decorated with birds' nests, road
maps, calling cards, menus, watch springs, swamp mari-
golds, spherical paper wasps' nests, flounder skeletons,
cat bones, little rubber horses, photographs of mine shafts
and skyscrapers. A printed pamphlet introducing the
spectacle was available on request. No dice. They sat
around and picked each other's noses and read the *Wall
Street Journal*. I even tried to improve club relations
with the farmers around here. I still had the Ferrari so
I could get to a lot of farms in a day. I would pull up
alongside a farmer, introduce myself as a member of the
Centennial Club and say, '*The earth is good, gentlemen.
Only the soil prevails.*' Then I would demonstrate eleven
thousand revolutions in all five gears just to keep their
attention, becoming as a tiny dot upon the green horizon.
What more could you ask? A living diplomat. I played
Teresa Brewer and Perez Prado records in the dining
room. Nothing. I gave away free ball-point pens and

trained Olson's dog to shake hands. I killed a rat. No response. Then I saw that rats and hats and ball-point pens weren't what it takes to electrify twenty-six thousand acres of forest and make it habitable. What it takes is tension and constant menace. And nothing overt would do. These birds can snuff out anything conventional with their various bribed public officials. My task has been to show them the grace and dignity of self-reliance through dueling so that they will think in terms of settling their own problems intramurally. Next I give them a problem. That's where Olive comes in and I expect he'll work out just right. Unless I miss my guess, he's raging around the forest like a rabid dog right now. That is a role Olson couldn't have fulfilled. He's too *realistic*. Now if they settle Olson's hash on their own they will have taken the first step in cutting themselves off from the outside, and the first step toward setting up a tiny enclave on the sensible systems of the Middle Ages."

"Who will be king?" Quinn said.

"Oh, come on. String along."

"I am. But who will be king."

"No king. It couldn't get that far. You can't run a single acre on the principles of the Middle Ages, much less twenty-six thousand. It would be a step toward destruction. That would suit me. I am sentimentally attached to these lands. And I have learned to be the enemy of the people that inherit them. That is what this club hasn't figured on—"

"What do you mean, Vernor? Come on, will you. Talk plain."

"Naw, suh! Dat's enuff. Ah has spoken."

Rather than dote on the latest Stanton pronunciamento, Quinn elected to spend the night fishing. As he prepared his tackle and made coffee for the thermos, he involuntarily thought of Stanton's insolent dream world and the cockeyed dramas that proceeded from it, commonly embroiling everyone around him.

Quinn headed for the river, not undertaking this fishing lightly. The night was warm and creaky, the round spring moon figured with bats and moths. He anticipated the hunting owls and raccoons rinsing mussels in the shallows; and the green luna moths of the spring fishing. He remembered how the long hours of staring at the mutable silky river often left him dazed for a day after. He wondered if this accounted for the seasonal drownings, fishermen turning up lodged under bridges or in log jams and having to be brought ashore with a boat hook; or those that simply vanished in still backwaters to rotate a couple of days before sinking. Such considerations dallied with his nerves when he was night fishing. Sometimes it only required a momentary loss of balance, the sound of feral dogs running deer or the whistle of the Pere Marquette railroad, and Quinn scrambled out of the river with a galloping case of the creeps to race up the grassy slopes to his house.

Quinn stepped into the dark river, already concentrating and beginning to sort out the sounds around him and to distinguish the musical splash of frogs from the slash of feeding trout and the careless splashy rises of young trout from the heavier, pulling rise of big fish; it all had to be done by ear. The darkness encouraged his dreaming and replaced Stanton's lunacies with heavy trout that threshed the smooth and moon-yellowed water. So far, there was no hatch of any kind; a few moths barged around and young trout slapped at mosquitoes. Raccoons hunted in the shallows and a black watersnake went by, carried sideways downstream, the head pointing steadily to the far bank while the tail drove. A good brown trout would eat a watersnake.

The river here was a hundred feet wide, fast and channeled along either bank. In the middle, two overlapping currents had built a gravel bar. Quinn was standing on this bar when he heard the blast. And because there is no part of the natural environment more constant than the sonic boom, he thought of that. But then he saw that this was denser and closer. It was dynamite. The silence in the blast's wake was severe. He waited instinctively. Then the water began to rise quickly around his knees and ahead of him he saw a low, glassy ledge hurtling in the moonlight toward him. An instant later, he was knocked flat under a cold swell of water that tore his rod from his hand and turned him hard against the cold gravel bottom helpless in his waders and off the end of the bar into the deep water of one of the channels where he shot along far beneath the surface, raked by the ends of sunken logs. He struggled with the waders, hauling them down around his knees, then fighting erect toward the surface for air and trying again until the waders were free of his legs and he thrust toward the top. But where the surface was to have been was only more water, black and intervening, and he compulsively filled his lungs and stopped struggling. The current ceased its swelling pressure and he hung a moment in black suspension feeling himself turn in some backwater. Then spasmodically he fought, punching and kicking into the blackness that yielded to him, deferred to him, until he found himself unexpectedly surfaced, then on a low ledge of mud that sank deeply under his hands and knees. He seemed to be reaching into the earth. He knelt sinking and expelled gouts of lung-warmed water in seizures of his chest. He lay down in the foul mud. A thick cloud of mosquitoes rose singing around him and settled again, covering him. He didn't resist, though he sensed dimly that they covered him and that the singing had stopped. He could feel, too, his lips pull away from his teeth in a grin, and a song repeat sonorously in his head as though sung in a culvert: "Dat ole black magic has me in its spell, dat ole black magic dat I know so well—" It was Stanton's voice. A few feet from Quinn's head the river hissed past. But where had that water come from, that whistling, glassy ledge of racing water? There was no flow control here as on the Manistee. He hadn't the energy to pursue it or to lift his limbs or resist the burning in his lungs. He couldn't wave away the mosquitoes that buried him.

Some time passed, probably hours, and Quinn awoke. It was very dark. The moon was invisible though its cold, chalky light hung over the trees. Quinn lifted his hands to his face. It was swollen and enormous. Bites had made its surface pebbly. He touched his lips and found them taut as the skin of a balloon. The sides of his finger pressed apart just as his mouth seemed to press open. Every move sent clouds of saclike mosquitos rising from his flesh and oscillating around him in soft waves of high-pitched sound. The river had fallen to normal and whispered past. Quinn got to his feet, sinking halfway to his knees in the mud, launching new clouds of mosquitoes up and streaming against the moonlight. He looked around himself. Everything was gone. His good rod was gone; he thought with helpless absurdity what a time he was having and how he had rewarded himself for a year's stupid labor. He felt solitary and ashamed at this moment of saurian floundering, muckbound helplessness and stupidity. All present hopes of pleasure were extinct and in their absence he thought he could make out the few, clear lines that kept himself, Stanton, Janey, everybody, precisely separated. The thought was subtle and insistent. Calamity had deprived him of his bland vacation. What remained, the accretion of the last weeks, was knowledge as clear as a simple geometric pattern, a few lines: final and sad.

3

CENTENNIAL MOON

H<small>E OPENED</small> the screen door, bumping his face as he went in, wandering through the wrong rooms on the ground floor of his own house before turning on lights and going upstairs to bed. On his back, his eyes hung from the ceiling light with its seamed, dusty, spilling glass cornucopia. His fingers beat with itching and he wanted to claw them, claw his beaded face and membrane lips. He got up and went to the sink and ran hot water on his hands for relief. Shortly after he lay down again, his view of the light was interrupted by the heads of Stanton and Janey. "What happened to you?"

"I was in the river. I was . . . knocked down by a wall of water."

Stanton said Olive had blown the dam and that it had all run down the tributary stream that drained it into the river. With one blast the lake had become a clearing. Dynamite. Stuff for blowing stumps. Stanton wanted to know what it was like, if it was exciting.

"A wall, I told you."

"You fortunate bastard. That was absolutely the last view of the lake anybody had." Janey said he looked sick.

"I am. I can't be brave. I've never felt this way before." He dozed off as though he were hurtling away and woke up a moment later in fear and lay in bed awake, feeling still a pull to hurtle into the night sky that tugged all around him elastically. He realized that the roar outside that seemed like wind was voices and he forced himself to get out of bed, feeling the pressure of his puffy feet run up his legs when his weight was on the floor. Turning the brass levers on the narrow-paned windows that stretched from floor to ceiling, he swung them down and stepped onto the narrow widow's walk where, in the daylight, the lake used to be visible. Below Quinn, directly in front of the porch, were all the men of the club. They were crowded together in a single unit. Fortescue stood in front of them, Scott behind. Except that the recruits already had guns, it would have looked like an induction center. Their lights and lanterns flashed and glowed and in every hand was a rifle of some kind: carbines, pump guns, doubles, Mausers. It was a man-hunt, a posse, and Quinn knew that it was poor Earl Olive, purveyor of live bait, who starred in the show. He studied them unsteadily. They were arguing. Fortescue was plunging an admonitory forefinger downward as though he had found oil, and Stanton, now below too, was cultivating a judicial air that was having no effect beyond irritation. Scott darted through the ranks shaping everyone up, and Murray led a small band in sentimental songs of the forties. Then Fortescue was finished, had forged these men into something of use, and they turned as a man and surged into the darkness with a roar of elation, their lamps flashing and working into the night. Quinn went back to bed, forgetting to turn out the light. He looked at it in despair, unwilling to get up again. When he opened his eyes it was morning and Janey was sitting beside a tall, shocking stripe of sky. Around her neck hung a pair of binoculars. Quinn's hands had perspired so much the skin felt tender and porous as though he'd been swimming. When Janey saw he was awake, she began to tell him about the night before: Earl Olive had got away.

Quinn remembered the beginning of the man hunt, remembered the rifles, lights, shouting. And through Janey he learned that that's all there had been, a beginning. The war party fording the first swamp, guns held crossways over their heads as at Parris Island, had, floundering and crying to each other for aid, heard, from behind, the successive dynamitings of each room of the main lodge; each explosion was louder than the one before either because of increasing charges or because the building had grown more sonorous with each gutting blast, each bellowing, plank-shattering cough of dynamite. Scott, according to Spengler, the chronicler, had, running about in confusion chest-deep in ooze, slogged a short way and vanished; dragged to high land, he had been mounted by Charles Murray who, Scott's fists unavailing, mouth-to-mouth resuscitated the little drenched antiquarian until Fortescue pulled him off and said, "Easy now. That'll do." Scott jumped up screaming in a gallinaceous rage that was quelled only by the return march to the compound where they viewed the ruins, the burst walls and tall rooms opened to the sky for the first time in the century. Fortescue walked around in front of his men and addressed them thus: "Gentlemen—" But his speech was precisely interrupted by a single small blast toward the lake. Fortescue, racing along behind the other men, swung his arm in a forward quarter-arc and cried "Follow me!" as they began to outdistance him. When they arrived at the lake, they found someone had dynamited the lifeguard tower; the seat had been blown fifty yards away and sat brightly on the dry lake bed. They decided to convene. They would have to devise some systematic mode of procedure; it was not to be expected that normally sedentary gentlemen should run up and down the countryside indefinitely. Fortescue moved to the fore. "Gentlemen—" he pleaded; but he was interrupted by a very small explosion from the direction they had come from and soon he was outdistanced by his companions. When they arrived again at the compound, they learned that the flagpole had been rather exactly dynamited. This time Fortescue began to screech. And Scott, now wearing a Mae West, tried to talk sense to him. But Fortescue continued to screech about advancing, flanking, fanning out and bivouacking. And when they'd got him under control, they had lost their momentum and began to think of getting some rest.

Quinn stared from the window. Where the blue lake had been in the trees was now a brownish green oval as sore as a roller rink. Clouds of crows whirled and flew, landed and fed on dead fish. Quinn took the field glasses and watched them plod over the lake bottom and pierce bloated trout with sudden thrusts of their heads. At the south end of the lake were the four rearing ponds that from this distance looked like ice trays. They still held water; but scrawny herons waded now and probed for young fish. To the left of Quinn's field of view, you could normally see the third story of the lodge; now nothing was visible, no wreckage, nothing at all, as though the building had reared up above the surface of trees for a few generations and sounded.

Quinn moved to Stanton's house, by his own request, where he could be more readily babied. They moved him into the spare room over the porch and he fell asleep instantly. When he awoke hours later, it was raining and Janey was there. The walls were invisible and the windows oblongs of dark-green ragged light. The weather made him daydream about Detroit, rain falling past office windows, rain stinking in the hearty woolens of Mary Beth, that Frankenstein, rain slanting into Woodward Avenue soaking shoppers in front of J. L. Hudson's, gleaming on Michigan Avenue, Gratiot, Grand River, soaking merchants, strikers, bozos, flaneurs, autodidacts, doughty young executives and hurrying shoppers holding packages to their breasts like praying mantises. Rain that here in the North rinsed dust from trees, in Detroit raised an unseen, mobile filth; it exaggerated the noise of traffic, made the headlights of cars stream and wheel and haunt the crevasses between buildings. But here at least it didn't seem like the last day there would be, the last emanation of gray light before the world went down gagging. Long spokes of sunlight already shot the clouds. "What are you waiting for?" Quinn asked.

"Nothing. What are you?"

"An older woman with a little something put aside."

"Really—"

"I don't know. Waiting for something to change." Beside him bacon, eggs and broiled tomatoes warmed in a silver chafing dish with a lamp beneath. He lifted the lid and looked in carefully. Janey wouldn't have any so he served himself on a square-handled salver. After that, Quinn dressed slowly while Janey watched out the window. Then they went to the compound to view the damage.

The destruction of the lodge was total. Only the plumbing stood out of the wreckage, white fixtures on pipe legs like mangrove hummocks. The cellar hole had begun to fill with water. The quantity of shattered lumber was astounding. In the compound there stood a huge carnival tent, now quite dark from rain. Around the entrance many club members were smoking and talking. The men were unshaven and disheveled. Quinn went inside with Janey. The rest of the membership was in here, their sleeping bags strewn over an acre or so of interior ground. There was a queer relaxation, a locker room air, people standing around in underwear, picking, fingering and itching at themselves. Something had gone with the buildings.

Quinn and Janey continued to walk through the tent even after the others had gone out to listen to Spengler read the prologue to his lecture. A man from the company that had supplied the tent was draining two great rain puddles that had formed overhead by incising them with a razor on the end of a twenty-foot bamboo pole. These dark ponds hung like blisters until the cut was made; then they vanished in a leaf of silver that hurtled to the floor where he mopped it up. Later, he would go aloft and stitch up the incisions.

They went outside and sat down. Quinn smelled the soaked ashes and embers, the clean pitch that had boiled out of the timbers of the lodge and been slaked with cold water. Spengler announced that he would in this time of crisis review the acquisition of club lands and summarize its social history with a view toward highlighting that spirit which went to make it the great institution which it was today. Stanton was heard to say, rather too audibly for comfort, "This ought to be good." The review began, the dreary account of acquiring the miles of both banks of the Pere Marquette that they had today. It soft-pedaled the succession of magnificent bribes that had been necessary (two greedy Presidents had clamored for ample lacings of this payola) to uproot the homesteaders and loggers who had settled in the area; when these hardheaded Scandinavians refused to move, no matter what papers or signatures were shown them, a feeling grew among the original club members that the intransigence of the hayseeds was criminally uncalled for; and that if they wanted to play rough, then play rough it was. Moreover, the founders decided, if, when push came to shove, these hicks tried to wave the Homestead Act of 1862 in their faces, then the founders would be obliged to sic the law on them. Open conflict set in and when the farmers appealed to decency, it was regarded as being neither here nor there, rather a canny bumpkin subterfuge not only not to be honored but not to be countenanced. Therefore, the reward of these farmers was entailment succeeded by dispossession. They were driven from the land, their minor prosperity undone and, to this day, unrecovered. They resettled close beyond club boundaries and their progeny and heirs produced the poachers and vandals that plagued the club today; they had produced Jack Olson for one.

They had land; now they needed buildings. At this time there was great interest in Indian life on the eastern seaboard and it was carried inland to Michigan through the efforts of a French scholar, secretary of the Choctaw Club of Lyons, who dressed in Indian garb and traveled about the U.S.A. after the Civil War, lecturing, drumming and dancing at fees that small communities could scarcely afford. These communities, therefore, began to interest themselves in local Indians, to collect "relics" and read romances of Indian life. The founders of the Centennial Club were not unaffected and they decided that the lodge would be built with Indian labor. They enlisted the aid of an Indian from Grayling who had been a sergeant in the Civil War and who had served as labor boss on many projects here in the North. He was an efficient and almost scrupulous foreman: he built the lodge in jig time, though his gang of Chippewa laborers, dressed by request in loin cloths and war bonnets, contained a number of white friends in disguise. This discovery was not made until the whites had done a certain amount of work which was impossible to isolate. So the main lodge went up incorporating a spiritual impurity which Spengler interpreted as a wedding of white and Indian traditions in the wilderness. He touched on the salient points of this tradition, the natural nobility of the savage, Shakespeare, Homer and whatnot; the rise of the American nation in the hands of such bush tycoons as the founders was accompanied by a kind of *temps perdu* of wigwam life. "Do you mean to tell me," Stanton inquired, "that all this gave way to make room for the *Centennial Club?*"

"That's what he means," said the still invisible Fortescue.

"Holy mackerel!" Against the northern sky the great lodge had taken shape. Swamp was made lake.

Was made swamp. (Stanton.) There was shelter, Indians, northern lights; in the beginning wolf and lynx challenged women, children, picnic tables. The founders dreamt of a better life, a place in the forest that would be safe for their own kind, for their hopes, their hibachi dreams. The forests flowed to the cities and financed such dreams. Timber cruisers goggled through white pine forests buying upland stands at swamp prices; not, mind you, the avaricious scuttling of unscrupulous lummoxes but straight Yankee ingenuity, a matter of being at the right place at the right time. The Centennial Club's lines thickened along the Pere Marquette. A lady wrote a three-thousand-line epic about it, now unhappily forgotten, called *Bogwhistle, a Song of the North*; it was in rhymed fourteeners with prose interludes that were read by her husband who played accompaniment on the concertina and passed the hat—"and put the blocks to her at night."

"Shut up, Stanton." Fortescue.

Janey said, "Have you ever been to Texas?"

"Just passing through."

"Where were you going?"

"I was going to Tulsa."

The speech went on. Quinn gazed at the distant back of Stanton's head, at its streaked sandy hair growing long; thought: Stanton experimented with haircuts, wore outfits, caught himself and paused at mirrors, dark windows; once asked people who they thought he was. At thirteen he bought rumba lessons with his allowance and wrote Captain Cousteau requesting citizenship in the first underwater city. What was he doing here?

Janey held out two hands together to match oval, pearly, imperfect nails as Spengler said that the general adaptation of the V8 by GM in '55 was a real shot in the arm for club revenues. "Good night!" said Stanton, bringing pause.

"You can't stop interrupting, can you?" said Fortescue getting to his feet visibly. "Can you?"

·"I thought this was audience participation . . ."

"Let me give you a little feedback here," said Fortescue. "You're a creep, Stanton. Have you got that? A creep."

"Mercy!"

What was Spengler starting now? He had pulled out a fresh load of notes, wrinkling them vertically and reflectively between his two hands as he looked across the tops of heads. Behind him a great panel of the tent filled and heaved with breeze. Stanton turned toward Quinn from up front, his face infuriatingly pear-shaped with mock solemnity. Quinn felt the jokes ricocheting obliquely away from him. His guilty preoccupations were all around. His company throbbed somewhere nearby, its buildings and offices linked like organs; behind, his mother gardened and his father fidgeted obesely in the Antillean sunlight; Stanton of course burned out there like an incendiary bomb. Then he thought of Earl Olive; or rather Olive appeared to him, coming up Stanton's darkened cellar stairs, his body rising through shadows like a smear, the scream whirling behind compressed lips as he came into the living room, his body shedding the darkness of the stairwell, assuming detail, the smudge that had been everything of him save his face becoming the chevron pockets of his western shirt, the five buttons at each wrist slit, the stylized mother-of-pearl horns on the plastic-eyed steerhead of his belt buckle; the buckle itself, embossed EARL, the size of a saucer; then from outside, past the knocking, open door, Olive's gnashing, reiterate howl of lunacy.

All of them—Spengler with his foul chronicle, Earl Olive sucking his paws in the woods, Stanton pouring salt in every handy wound, Fortescue leading his squad up and down the hill between explosions like Pavlov's dogs, Quinn and Janey soft-shoeing it around one another—all of them seemed to move away from each other like lines on a globe that would converge invisibly beyond. But maybe too that point of convergence would be a fantastic dogfight or Western-movie saloon debacle replete with screaming frontier twats, bloodied heads, breakaway chairs, collapsing shelves of bottles. Why not? Already the physical ruin of the club was past comprehension. A lake over seventy years old that had become part of the general memory of the county's wildlife was a suppurating mudbowl. And it was Quinn who had seen the lake last, moving like an express train on its glassy trajectory down the Pere Marquette. But what still astonished him was the readiness for calamity there had been in the air. Even the shed with its compact wooden boxes of dynamite lying waxed and fuseless in rows convenient to the land must have longed for use. Then the aftermath was a hangover; indulgence shrunk away to nothing; everyone was stopped, wooden; only Earl Olive was at large, functional, decisive and arbitrary as a child or goblin. Quinn reflected upon Olive, calling up only a few traits: his considerable size, his wide cheekbones, the mouth the distant corners of which each indicated a small, low ear; and of course the hair, long but close like the hair of a puppet. ". . . the assignment of club finances to professional management in the late fifties . . ."

"*Dum de da dum,*" Stanton hummed aggressively.

"May I go on?"

"If you can," Fortescue said to Stanton who looked at him, raised open palms and silently mouthed the word, "Me?" This small gesture struck Fortescue in the face like a blow. A suffusion of red flashed and the perimeter of white around his eyes grew wide. Quinn fought to keep from awarding Stanton points for this precise and economical shot.

When Spengler finished what was only the prologue of his chronicle, he asked for comments from the floor; and Scott said he hoped that in his final treatment Spengler would "flesh out" what had merely been suggested in the introduction. Spengler answered, "Clearly," and Scott rising to the tacit challenge and in fact getting himself into something of a snit suggested that the prose could stand a little "pruning" too, a little "cleaning up" if not actual "reworking" from "stem to stern."

"You could pay attention," Stanton said to Spengler; "this man is a pro and he's good."

"I thought I made it clear that this was an early draft."

"Darn it, you did," said Stanton, turning to Scott. "Professor Scott, I would have thought your experience down there at Moo U., if you'll pardon the expression, would have taught you a little flexibility. What say you give old Spengler a fighting chance?" Fortescue interrupted Scott's reply.

"We don't need a moderator," he said. "We can do without one."

"Then shut up," said Stanton.

"Look—"

"Or get out. Pack."

Janey's fingers closed around Quinn's arm.

"*What* do you mean?" Fortescue said after a minute. One felt behind the mad spaniel face legions of tiny soldiers.

"I mean simply this: in a larger and more irritating sense you've been moderating this whole club and I for one am bored with it. The solutions I have indicated have been shutting up or getting out. I don't know how much clearer I can make it, Mister Fortescue. But I'll say this: I won't be interrupted by you again. You're a bore, you're a professional phony and for the twenty years I've watched you strut around here it has been all I could do to keep from booting you right in the seat of your smug and comfortable pants." Spengler and Scott were gone. The others, folding blankets, broke up too and were gone.

Fortescue turned undamaged on his heel and vanished into the black pentagram of the tent's entrance. More would be heard from that quarter. Stanton followed unhappily after. Quinn wondered what was changing him. This had been the painful fetching up of purest bile; and if that was so, why did he do it? Was it an airing of old resentments, as he said; or had he linked these activities too with abstractions? Because it wasn't funny and because it could be seen as the beginning of a new and more menacing form of irresponsibility, Quinn used it to imagine himself intervening to protect Janey, then taking her away for her own good.

A cycle of these ran through Quinn's mind: he bolts with her in a car, an airplane, a Pullman; then she is before him as she had been in the clearing that afternoon; now, he himself stands over her with rifle and bowie knife, eyes thinned by the line of horizon, slowly shifting like radar, without carnal inclination. The girl at his feet could be a piece of precious statuary. Suddenly the vision is replaced by one of Lu, pissing in the weeds then wandering off, butt aloft and splayed like that of a plucked turkey. Toying with himself like this was deliciously painful. Janey had become a sweet emotional abscess; it was exquisite to touch the knife to it.

Back in the room in Stanton's house, he gazed weakly and bravely through the high window. He was in bed now, his hands crossed on his chest. Janey had made a sick boy's meal for him of sandwiches and bouillon with a pot of strong black tea. He nipped at the sandwich's delicate edge and thought, Am I the one? A plastic transistor radio on the windowsill whispered *"I'm a hog for you, baby"* to the solid oink and snuffle of a Detroit blues band. He studied her, studied the perfect lateral movement of her eyes. He wondered if he moved his own as characteristically; he had learned making faces in the mirror that you never saw your own eyes move; this crucial detail was forever a mystery to the narcissist. Too bad. It explained a lot; for instance, in Janey it showed her care as a listener: in that lateral motion was attention and consideration. Quinn was pleased to have isolated it. He looked around the room that seemed as fresh as a newly drained spring. What was all this glee about? He sat straight upright, heedless of the headboard. "Did you ever have a job?" he asked.

"Had a lot of jobs."

"Such as?"

"I was a model, a librarian, a guide in a champagne factory."

"You were? Where was that?"

"It was the only champagne company in Waco and it wasn't a good job. I took thirty tours a day and made the same speech over and over. The tour started upstairs where it was usually about a hundred degrees and it ended up in the cellars fifty degrees colder. So, I always had the grippe until I demanded to be put upstairs or down. They put me downstairs. My job was to rotate the bottles so the residue would settle evenly. I had to wear a fencing mask in case a bottle blew up. I got pneumonia and went back to the mineral spring."

"Do you plan to get married?" Quinn asked, his eyes traveling over slatted, white-painted walls with their

155

streaks of paint beading. Janey was biting her cheek again. Quinn reached and pushed her chin with his forefinger to make her stop.

"Well!" she said. "If I could do it right!"

"What kind of wife would you make?"

"A good one!"

"I'd marry you myself," Quinn said, wrapped up in his own fraudulence.

"Well, I wouldn't marry you!"

"Why not?" He was still looking at boards, fixtures and chairs, a real interior decorator. Janey was no longer biting her cheek. And Quinn felt that he had to explain who he was and that he could do it quickest by indirection, by talking about the hats he had worn, cars he had owned, the women he had been with, the fly rods he used, the profits he had made. It worked in the past; why wouldn't it work now? It wouldn't work now. He knew that by instinct.

". . . then a funny thing happened," Janey said, still thinking and now smoking and clicking a gold Dunhill lighter in her hand. "Vernor and I would be . . . I wonder . . . okay, Vernor and I would be walking in the street . . ." She went very carefully. Stanton had been getting strange, insisting that people were "cruising" him. They had to leave restaurants before they'd eaten because he had spotted people outside the window cruising him. After that—and this was all after Quinn had last seen him—he got worse. He wrote sarcastic letters to his father who was dead. He started traveling, taking Janey along, at an absurd rate, a country or two a day. One peculiar thing, a rude clerk or some tourist cruising him, as he saw it, and they had to get out. He spent less than five minutes in Spain after seeing a dwarf in a flowerprint sport shirt slumbering with a bright strip of lottery tickets pinned to his chest. *"Did you see that?"* he had demanded. *"Did you?"* They were in Gold Beach, Oregon, the next day, where Stanton couldn't stand the smell of fish because it was an airborne river of lethal botulism. Everywhere they went, the mail mania dominated: he had to have letters. They tried Florence the year before the floods and saw men throwing treble hooks in the swollen Arno for bodies and Stanton screamed at the draggers in bad Italian demanding to know who they thought they were. That one ended with the police and jail, where Stanton couldn't get the mail without enormous bribes once the local officials had matched his bankroll with his psychosis. Quinn thought of the letters he had planned but never written to Stanton; he saw Stanton before him in the fluorescence of advanced personal decrepitude. Janey handed him a calling card; on one side was Stanton's name; on the other it said, "No, prisoners of love, I did not begin as a joke." After Florence, Stanton began to invent conversations which he would write down and then memorize. He made Janey learn cues so that when people were around she could lead him from one recital to the other. She would give him one line and he would talk for five minutes and she'd give him another. Some were about Quinn. Some about Judy, the aunt; some about his father. Quinn asked what the other speeches were: a short history of the exploration of the Nile, a lecture on how the first zippers were made, instructions for building a Bessemer converter or making sourdough bread. When people got bored, he really buried them. One day, they were sitting in a German restaurant in Philadelphia and he leaned over and whispered that he could no longer move his arms and legs. They got him into a clinic right away. He called his mother in Michigan and she told him to pull himself together. He had to be watched every minute. He said his lanyard had snapped. He said his life had gotten to be so funny he couldn't stand the laughing. He said his spring was running down and that the whole mechanism would have to be returned to Switzerland for adjustment. They carried him into the clinic like a plank and the psychiatrist attending him said that he was exaggerating the little things we all have. Quinn listened and looked on with new regard and a hopelessness that would have cleared the air if he had accepted it.

The discovery that Earl Olive was a criminal and a fugitive should have surprised nobody; but it surprised Quinn. Fortescue, visiting the ailing young businessman with an eye to enlisting his aid, bent his authoritarian spaniel face to a teletyped dossier and, scanning, gave Quinn a rapid précis of its contents: fraud, arson, assault and battery, breaking and entering, suspicion of armed robbery, suspicion of rape, suspicion of murder, known to be armed, considered dangerous. The fraud conviction began as a rape indictment, Fortescue explained, his eyes scanning another stapled pair of sheets. Earl Olive had been in the habit of calling up girls he didn't know and representing himself as a social worker; it had been his practice to explain confidentially that they had been established as V.D. carriers and would have to be treated under state supervision. At this point, the girls were willing to accept Olive's help: he would recommend a friend with rare type-M-positive blood who could stop the disease through sexual intercourse; the girls were eager for this simple cure; and Olive, "the friend," would soon be at the door. It was only that the girls stayed on for more than the prescribed treatment that forced the disillusioned judge to change the indictment to the charge of fraud. Olive was convicted. He jumped bail and went on with the crimes that continued out there in the woods.

"Why don't you call the police?" Quinn asked sensibly.

"Why do you think? Because we clean our own house here."

"Seems pointless."

"Does it? It doesn't to me. There are still some of us alive for whom life in the forest means a return to older virtues, not just a vacation."

"Very well, if you want to make a speech."

"I mean you and your friend Stanton and the rest of your generation are just a little farther away from the founding years of this country."

"Mm, being younger."

"And we're not sarcastic and we're not facetious and damn it there are things we call valuable. What I'm saying is that we believe we can clean this Olive business up in a way that will not only be a tribute to the Centennial Club but a tribute to the country as well."

"It sounds like you have your hands full."

"So don't tell me police."

"I see now I was playing the wrong shot. Gee—"

"I've got equipment rolling in now, paid for out of my own pocket, I might add. I got a rack of Winchester riot guns, K-rations, rucksacks, primus stoves, hammocks, a quartermaster's tent for extended bivouac, compasses, aerial photographs, flares, tracers."

"Any grommets?"

"Well, the tents have grommets on their corners. What do you mean! Anyhoo, are you with us or agin us?"

"Oh, agin you, I would say."

"Then stay out of the way. That's an order."

When it was dark, Quinn crept through the compound in his bathrobe, feeling a little sick and unsteady in the night. He went around and around the tent, each time cutting one more strand of the powerful guy ropes that held the tent aloft. In the vague light that came from within, the tent was a glacier. Quinn paused once in this superior task and had a giddy moment of not knowing where he was; when it came to him again, as it did immediately, he saw himself as a resistance fighter, a saboteur with ideals. Then he went on with his cutting until halfway around the tent on perhaps the fifth pass, one of the guy ropes popped; then they all went like a zipper and the great tent slumped. Quinn ran for it, running in a sick blur, as oaths and cries raged from under cloth; and by the time he was well into the woods, the riot guns were barking importantly into the night.

Back in his sickroom, the bed itself seemed to reject him like the trick-shop miniature of King Tut. Quinn thinks: *I am in it hand and foot. I have suffered a relapse.*

In the morning, in bed, Quinn still in Stanton's house and posturing sickly for Janey, Charles Murray appeared.

He had a bouquet wrapped in wax paper and a packet of letters. "Yoohoo," he said, "couldn't you hear me knocking away? I've been to the mail in town today—" He handed Quinn his letters, then shyly, "—these silly old—" Janey got up to get them coffee and Quinn followed her exit with forlorn eyes. He held the flowers now; they were dark orange. "How are you feeling?" Murray asked.

"Oh, all right."

"You probably have the *flu* for God sakes."

"I know, I know. But this was kind." Quinn waved the flowers awkwardly. Murray brushed off the compliment.

"They're just tacky nothings. All you can expect up here though. You do look feverish." He laid his narrow hand on Quinn's brow.

"I feel pretty much terrific," Quinn said abruptly.

"After what you've been through? How killing!"

"Just a little dunking—"

"A little dunking!" He seized Quinn's hand in wild laughter. Quinn tugged a tiny bit but was held fast. Murray leaned over. "What the hell?" he squinted.

"What do you mean?" Murray relinquished his hand and threw his own in the air. "Oh, how should I know, how should I *know!* So much is happening so fast! My poor brain is no better than a big silly Caesar salad!" His face flushed and he turned into the wall close by and simpered, "Really, it's insupportable. Well!" He jumped up. Janey came in. "I've got to go! I have a date with an angel! Janet Fortescue by name!" He and Janey dodged and feinted in the doorway before Murray got away, Quinn calling out his thanks after. An instant later, farther down the stairs, Stanton could be heard gruffly

161

and rudely putting Murray on. His own approach was not secretive, the drumming of heavy footwear on a hollow staircase, no doubt exaggerated in its regularity; and his entrance, pausing in the doorway, a big grin behind the white linen handkerchief into which he trumpeted majestically; then rolling the cloth, he thrust it into his hind pocket. Quinn suddenly felt their quietude and inactivity in the contrasting presence of Stanton. Stanton was noble in knee-high black Wellingtons and green turtleneck pullover. His mouth opened fiercely and he gave lung to a great elk roar. "Well, sir," he said softly, "I like to give you what you expect."

"And thank you."

"What's the talk up here? Cultural topics?"

"I'm afraid you were the subject in question."

"I saw Murray on the way in. What'd he have in mind?"

"He was visting me."

"Figured on getting a little, did he?"

"The question never came up."

Stanton's mouth found its natural downward curve though his eyes continued to hunt in their old troublemaking way. "The rampant Olive struck again last night. He collapsed the tent with the whole club inside—" Quinn began to laugh in childish yelps. Stanton laughed too, then stopped and began to hunt with his eyes again. "Wait, there's more. I know, Quinn, but shut up, can't you? Fortescue was adjusting one of the inside lines and he had it around his waist for purchase. When the tent collapsed and the center pole went down, it snatched him forty feet. Fortescue is a madman. He's shooting everything that moves, sending up flares. He is crazed and he's got rope burns all over his body. His wife tried to take the riot gun away from him and he slapped her face like a punching bag. It has gone nuts over there. Fortescue screams orders like the D.I. and everyone wants to go home but they're afraid to. Fortescue won't let them. He imagines word will leak and the police will be in on it. They've propped up the canvas with timber to make a ledge and they're living under it. Twenty-four-hour watches. On top of that they're still going to have the centennial celebration on the Fourth and dig up that fucking time capsule. God, Quinn, won't you join me? Please! We could make it so insane for those bastards!"

"What about Olive?"

"I know, I know, mmmm. In some ways, I'd like to plug him. Would too, if I could be sure of not killing him. Hate to go to the pen over that kind of riffraff. And that's what Olive and his crew are: riffraff, marginal types, floozies, shabby local farm stock—" This version grated Quinn. Stanton, it seemed, had watched the Olive camp with field glasses. He was an authority.

Janey asked, "What do they do?"

"They serve Olive. He's forcing the men to build a big lodge out there. He himself does not work. Now and again he drags one of the women off into the bush. You can bet it comes to no good, too." Quinn imagined the demented bait purveyor demanding his perquisites of Lu, throwing his hairy, bellied person on her little smudged body. Quinn wondered if, peaceful and tired, she whizzed on the ground after Olive had done with her, flicking leaves over the spot with backsweeps of her feet as dogs will do. Quinn saw Lu when she had been his alone, smiling wanly in the half-light with her behind looking like nothing so much as a pair of pale coughdrops or a papier-mâché valentine; and he could share Stanton's antipathy. "They sing together," Stanton said with vituperation.

"What kind of songs?"

"Couldn't make it out. They had a little fire and they swayed and moved their mouths—"

"Vernor," Quinn said, "what's the use? It hasn't anything to do with you."

"Yes it has, Parson Quinn. What you don't see is that it's a moral issue."

Quinn thought that this time he really had his chin out.

"Don't give me the business," Quinn said. "Just tell me why you're going after everybody."

"Because I hate it all."

"You hate it all."

"I hate it all."

"And what do you love?" Quinn was sick of Stanton's spleen.

"Janey and my father. Only he's dead. And when he was alive he complicated things by staying ninety-nine percent dead drunk. Then there was you. But you became a smug and irritable prick and a cheap bourgeois. I take it back. There, too much talk induces a shooting off of the mouth."

"Keep it up. Keep talking, God damn you."

"Aren't you getting a little imperious in your sickbed?"

"No."

"Seems your recent years with the Detroit business

castrati have made you overconfident. Now don't get me started, James; because I'm not going to mess with you once I do." Placid, malevolent tones: Quinn listened to them, felt Stanton's real strength in laying down the law.

"Don't hold yourself back," Quinn said, his mind already gliding from Stanton to Janey to his business to the unopened letters in his lap, to the two armies outside his window; Janey looked on and everything he learned about her saddened him and irritated him. He didn't want his women, it seemed, to be persistent; he wanted them delicate, frangible, dissolving, unreal. Rapunzel growing her hair to the ground from her high castle window had become in Quinn's mind bare-bummed behind, invisibly assaulted while she turned false, soulful eyes to the ground and awaited the prince who could clear everything up by using the backstairs.

But the exchange with Stanton reminded him of old days when one of the weekly fights would flare and Stanton would surprise Quinn with real attempts to injure him, times when his eyes were cold and occupied with the task of injury, the estimates of coordination needed to direct injury. And the surprise was always abrupt because the fights grew out of a closeness that made ideas pass between them in assured symbiosis, conversations become long conceits cross-referred to conversations months earlier, overblown, fantastic and serene. An enormous world constructed from within, hermetic as it was reassuring—Quinn had relinquished it slowly and unwillingly as Stanton's ambitions shaped him beyond expectation.

"Ah, well," Stanton was talking, "why should we argue about who pushes dis shabby organization obah de cliff. All dem desperate creeps, all dat disposable humanity."

"Why do you have to cultivate your mean streak," Janey asked.

"Oh, *dat*," said Stanton smiling. "I do dat natchally!"

Stanton left the room and hardly had time to get away from the house when they heard him being shot. A long moment later, he appeared once more in the room and collapsed on his stomach, blood spattering the green turtleneck pullover. When in the midst of suitable confusions the pullover was removed, they saw that his back was speckled with rocksalt, an old and popular stunt by bloody-minded local farmers, more insulting than dangerous. When Stanton learned this, though he writhed nonetheless, he was disgusted he hadn't followed his original plan. And in a moment, he had rushed out again and been shot again and there was that much more doctoring to be done, disinfecting merely, for the salt would dissolve out, painfully cleaning its own wound. Quinn strained his eyes at the window to see who was doing the shooting, shouted "*I see you, now get!*" into the darkness and was rewarded by the crack of a shotgun and the rattle of salt against the shingles. "Can't we please get out of here?" asked Janey sensibly and calmly. "Can't we?"

"No!" crabbed the prostrate, speckled Stanton from the bed Quinn had occupied so recently. "We cannot." Quinn noticed the sharply proprietorial air of Stanton now drawing beneath his chin the edge of the thick tan blanket and reclining like a stone mortuary figure. It appeared to Quinn that there would be the matter of his finding another place to stay and recuperate because he would not fight for the bed. Still, he felt, completely apart from the events themselves, that he'd been had. Stanton was speaking: ". . . I said to the man invisible in the dark but doubtless either Olive himself or one of his henchmen, said as clearly as I could, 'Shoot if you must this old gray head' and BOWANGO! they ripped into me with a raking broadside! Whiskey." Janey gave him the bottle from under the window seat and a glass. "What about rubbing alcohol for the afflicted areas."

"There is none."

"None? Why not?"

"There never was any—"

"Use it up on Quinn?" he laughed through locked teeth. "What the Christ, every man should have a fifth column in his home. I'm as *moderne* as anybody. But for God sakes, if a man is to go to the wars he ought at least to be left his medicine. I would think the subject was treated in international agreements."

Aggressive and ironic, Quinn never knew how to meet this line of Stanton's. Anyone who sat silent and un-objecting was a victim; anyone who retaliated, a spoil-sport, humorless. Quinn, neither one, floated in uncom-fortable liberty. "May I sleep downstairs?" he asked.

"Absolutely, absolutely."

"In the morning, I'll go to my own place."

"You be the judge of that. However, don't count on Janey for any services. She'll be right busy, understand?"

Quinn wouldn't even answer this one. He knew that unless he deferred to Stanton on a kind of yassuh-boss basis, it would be necessary to make a run for it to his own house. One look at Stanton's perforated dorsal, rendered painless though it was through subjugation to larger lunacies, made Quinn fear such a dash and he hesitated before picking up his grip and telling Stanton what a shit-ass he was.

"Scurrile," replied Stanton. Quinn shot his eyes to Janey, apologetic for his childishness. Her hands and crisscrossed fingers lay in her lap exactly as they had in the photograph of the Cotton Bowl game.

"Let me know," she said with contrition and more helplessness, "if there is anything I can do. At all."

"Fine. Thank you. I think I'll be going to my place."

"Back to the house is it?" Stanton inquired.

"If I can."

"You can do it."

"What's that?"

"Go back to your house. You can do it." Stanton's eyes flickered beneath heavy lids.

"I said that I would. Weren't you listening?"

"Moral support was all I could offer. I can't carry you home now."

"Stay downstairs, why don't you," Janey suggested. Quinn wanted to and would have if Stanton's face swollen with smugness hadn't challenged even that amenity.

"Drink your Bosco," Stanton called. "Bye-bye."

Leaving the house at all, required a couple of familiar ploys. He whistled conspicuously behind the closed porch door a moment and opened it thrusting an overcoat and hat on a broomhandle into the space. These objects were not fired upon and Quinn went on his way home. He went directly through on the path, and around him the tree trunks stood like the ribs of a sunken ship, their spaces exaggerated by the clear moonlight. He stopped. He had no desire to return to his empty house. After the proximity of Janey, the steady sound of their voices still in his mind, the thought of the empty wooden building seemed depressing to the point of being ominous. He began to head crosslots toward the compound. In a moment, he came to the lake and walked to its edge. The sun had baked away much of its foul odor. There was nothing to encourage Quinn's memory. Even the dock, still standing, seemed unfamiliar. Before, it had lain inches above the unfluctuating surface of the lake; now it towered high on its pilings above half a dozen canoes sprawled morbidly below. Quinn walked on till he came to Stanton's cutter. He ran his hands over the high runners and tested the flexion of its double-sprung seat with his hand. Then he wandered out onto the lake bed. Long aquatic weeds were stretched upon its surface and dried fast; they looked like the silhouettes of trees and in the moonlight retained a green pallor. The lake bed itself was dried out and its surface deeply fissured, lunar and dead. On a plateau behind the far edge of the lake, Quinn perceived the glow of the club's lights and made for them. About midway, he came upon the horse, stretched out as Stanton had said, like an arrow: head reaching, legs trailing. The bones were white, almost luminous in the moon, and among the ribs, which stood up far higher from the lake floor than the rest of the skeleton, were metal harness fittings. Quinn sat astride the skeleton, smiling bleakly, and his legs outstretched in front of him as though he were on some outlandish Flexible Flyer; he gripped the short ribs in his hands and could see before him the barrel of the rib cage like white slats in the moonlight, trailing to the single heavy whiteness of the skull which, stretching forward from the streamlined limbs, made Quinn feel already that he was in motion; so much so that when he tilted his vision slightly above the treetops he lost all reference and the stars streamed behind like foam; he unconsciously tightened his grip on the ribs and let his head fall back so far that his mouth opened and the velocity of the stars increased until they overtook themselves in a whitening that became the moon. Quinn tilted his head down to the steadying serration of trees and got up. He crossed the lake bed to the plateau beyond. He went a very short distance from the edge of the plateau and found himself looking down at the unpleasant ventilation sleeve of an automatic rifle. The muzzle and front sight of the weapon were pressed invisibly into his belly. "It's you, Quinn," said Spengler, withdrawing the gun.

"What is this?"

"I'm on sentry."

"Is that loaded?"

"Of course it's loaded."

"For what?"

"It's loaded to shoot. What do you think it's loaded for? What do you load a gun for?"

"I don't."

"Sure you do. What d'you mean? Everybody loads a gun." Quinn looked at Spengler's harmless, unlined face, flush with craziness, and asked him how the sentry duty was being administered. Spengler laughed at this word.

Fortescue, he said, would point a finger: you're it. It wasn't, Spengler insisted, the fairest thing in town. The snivel had become recognizable. "A big boy like you," Quinn said and thought Spengler would break down.

"Lay off," he said. Quinn ignored him.

"Well, what's the plan? Is anybody ever going home?"

"When we clean up here, I guess. When we celebrate the centennial and dig up the time capsule and take care of the Olives—" What did taking care of them mean? Did it mean turning them over to the law as it did not seem to mean? Or did it mean something more direly in the vigilante line? It was too easy to picture Lu, the fat girl, the motorcyclist and their companions, all in a line that began with Olive, strung up on a limb down in the swamp they now inhabited. "What do you mean by taking care of them?"

"I—don't—know." Spengler stood firmly by his ignorance. No one ever knew about such things; not completely; maybe a little; enough of them knowing a little but not completely and you had the deed without the consequences; that's right, gentlemen, no hangover, no morning after. "Quinn, do yourself a favor and get out, would you?"

"I'm a member."

"What?"

"I'm a member."

"So what?"

"This is my club. I'm a member and I won't get out."

"Kid—"

"I won't get out."

"Kid, lissename—" Spengler's Brooklyn accent was

171

brand new. "There's a hundred million bums in a world, will ya lissename?"

"Give me that gun."

"Not on your life."

"Give me the gun or I'll take the gun and kill you with it." Spengler gave him the gun. "I have a good mind to kill you with this."

"What'd I ever do to you?"

"Stuck it in my belly. I ought to kill you and burn your chronicle."

"I didn't mean anything by it. I treated you like a Dutch uncle. Honest."

"I've got a good mind to cream your guts all over the bushes."

"Oh, don't even talk like that—"

"I'm sick of what's going on around here." Quinn was glad to have the gun. Spengler was crazy all right. Maybe now he would go home. Quinn wondered how many of these zanies were similarly armed. He looked over at Spengler, very much down in the mouth, his brief time in the military sun a thing of the past. Quinn gave him a little bump on the shoulder with his fist just to show that it would be fine again one day, that things would turn out like old times. Quinn unloaded the gun and went up. He found Fortescue polishing his boots outside the canvas ledge and lifted his head with the end of the automatic rifle. Fortescue's expression of cynicism tightened and confirmed itself. "So you've gone over—"

"No." Quinn leaned the gun up against the canvas and hunkered near Fortescue.

"Where'd you get the gun?"

"I had it, see?"

Fortescue's eyes flicked over it once.

"Just like the ones I got from the National Guard."

"Well, it's a common enough gun," Quinn said sharply.

"Still and all—"

Quinn noticed people beginning to treat him with respect. A heavy woman in desolating, elasticized underwear stepped out from under the ledge and emptied a pot; she paused odiously, her back to them, one hand behind her stretching a rubber strap absentmindedly, then lifted her head to ogle the firmament. There was the harsh scent of the pot's contents. The light of lanterns, stoves, cooking fires, flashlights, flickered out from under the ledge as Quinn went along. Among the members, Quinn spotted a few old woodsmen, local guides hired on as mercenaries. The guides were doing the cooking and thrusting out sections of the unwieldy canvas on green poles to form flies under which you could be sheltered.

Everyone visible seemed weary. Of these, the most voluptuously weary was Charles Murray. His weariness was of the staring, fixed variety that one associates with trench warfare on the old Western Front; you saw in his eyes the blind light of phosphor and star shells over a barbed-wire no man's land; you saw night raids that featured the bayonet and its use. But instead of sappers and subalterns you saw cranky children on a hot July night with mothers and fathers throwing themselves into sudden squalor with slackness that would have appalled Gypsies. Fortescue caught up with him again. "Naturally the camp is in confusion. You might say that at this stage of the proceedings confusion is necessary and desirable. Strategic even. Operationally, we're right on schedule."

"I didn't ask you to explain yourself."

"Oh, boy."

"What do you want with Earl Olive anyway? What are you going to do with him?"

"Interrogate him."

"After that?"

"First we're going to interrogate him and then we're going to interrogate him."

"Give him a little of his own."

"All right."

"And you think that's okay."

"All right, sure. We think it's okay."

"A tit for a tat."

"There you go," said Fortescue emphatically. "Now you're getting real close to what we have in mind."

"Well, here's one from left field: I won't allow it."

"What can you do?"

"Turn you over to the authorities."

"Like who?"

"Like the sheriff of Pere Marquette," Quinn said promptly. "The sheriff of Pere Marquette—" It was sonorous.

"I can be of some use there," said Fortescue. "I am his deputy." He showed the card in its plastic panel, the wallet fanned with celerity. "Why don't you call on me? I am deputy or assistant chief to every law enforcement officer in this part of the state of Michigan. Why not call on me and see if I can't solve your problem?"

"I guess you've got me."

"I guess I've got you by the nuts."

Stanton answered: "I am always ready to present Mr. Earl Olive, address unknown, with his choice of weapons. Only fair thing to be done. I perhaps overcredit Sir Olive. That is to say that I don't think he would do the same for me. In fact, I'm confident that something in the back would be more his line of products. Not that I would fear that. When a man's up to his blowhole in the higher virtues, he cannot be stopped by weaponry. I expect to be among those savages within the hour, a trusted if shopworn student of their revolution." He was repacking his rucksack now and sat on his heels before it. He pressed into it skillfully a lightweight sleeping bag, a nested aluminum cook kit, an assortment of freeze-dried food, brown rice, fruit salad, vitamin supplements, Milky Way candy bars, a compass with a rotating dial, a pint of cognac, a pair of dueling pistols, a pair of dirks, a pair of short swords, *On Your Own in the Wilderness* by Bradford Angier and a manual of guerrilla tactics by Ernesto "Che" Guevara. "I'll see you on the Fourth of July."

"That's tomorrow."

"So it is. Let's do our club and country proud."

"I see that we will."

Quinn went to see Janey. He believed that if he kept showing up, something would break, an old delusion that substituted exposure for action. He took his time. It seemed so quiet. The old generator at the main lodge was silent now and it made an extraordinary difference. It had dominated a thousand acres of forest like a rhythm section. Now he felt the difference between this place and the world he lived in. It had taken a long time to shed Detroit; but once shed, it seemed uncannily remote. Not that he had forgotten the disaster that awaited him for failing to arrange the factory picnic or for ignoring the accounts Mary Beth was antagonizing; but still Detroit seemed remote enough that Quinn had to use his imagination to believe that any other life than this transpired; he didn't altogether believe that his punch presses and toolmaking machines still cavorted in their mechanical ecstasies, that his employees shuffled beside them, that Mary Beth still typed away between lunch hour assignations. He was not now even sure that his father snuffed cigarettes with sausage fingers in the blind West Indian sun, that his mother shook her head four times a year over his father's cardiogram and tried to talk him out of raiding back to Detroit to bully, wheedle and cajole the company into spasms of output and profit; for Quinn, it had all stopped; there was only this life and its details: he had adapted as animals adapt when they learn to live in a zoo, to eat, sleep and breed under a shower of peanuts and popsicle wrappers.

He looked up to see Janey in the highest window. She beckoned and he trotted toward the house thinking, What in the name of God, can this be it? The steps sailed by three at a time and he was in the room. Janey waved him past to the window. He took the binoculars from her in disappointment and looked, moving them back and forth. Rivers of green poured into each eye.

He elevated the glasses to the fissured brown of the lake. There he was. He was dancing on the lake bed with great seriousness, his jaw pressed against his chest, his underlip thrust out; he flapped his arms with a slow condor motion while his feet carried his scurrying in widening gyres. Suddenly, he threw his head back and Quinn was sure he imitated the cry of some raptorial bird. Then he put the rucksack back on and moved away with the heavy fluency of a prizefighter. The man's a loony, thought Quinn as he turned to Janey; will that clear the air? Scarcely. She thought it was funny. Quinn wanted to make her see that people didn't live like this; but what was the use. No one was going to get her away from Bird Man out there.

Whatever, Stanton was what Quinn and Janey had in common. So he talked to her now about everything that seemed to bear upon Stanton's present conduct. Once Stanton told him that he liked it when the tension was up and that was all right; he said that there were a few occasions when his entire brain was in full function and that it was for these moments he lived. Quinn could believe that too; trouble came through the means he chose to achieve this end. Coming back from Bermuda, the daughter of a mountain states beer baron told him that he was using his fruit fork on his fish course; Stanton bellowed a filthy rejoinder. Then, rising in a silence that seemed to expose the noise of air molecules colliding, he said, to the entire contents of the first-class dining room, "You have guessed it. I am a drug fiend," walked to the door, said, "Why should I hide it any longer? I'm on the stuff. It is as a sickness." He turned to the door—it was the service door—passed through anyway, tested sauces, frostings, a soufflé batter, plucked the chef's cheek and complimented him for being a wizard, a *wizard*, went up on deck and apostrophized the sea in stentorian tones. He then returned quietly to the first-class dining room, where his under-pressure charm dissuaded the captain from a ship's arrest, and ruefully assured his companions at table that opium was an ancient vice to which he was congenitally liable; certainly his mother's family, the De Quinceys, should answer for *that*.

Other officials had been less easy to convince than the captain. His many jailings had forced Harvard to redefine its relationship with civil law; the problem was exercised first at large among the undergraduates, then at the law school and finally in the offices of those who directed the institution. *"I'm on pins and needles!"* Stanton was heard squealing and the phrase had a resurgence of popularity. Finally, it was ruled the civil standing of a hooligan or petty criminal would have nothing to do with his academic standing; and Stanton remained to graduate.

When he was young, Stanton was most insistent about matters of right and wrong; of this there is a prime example: The members discovered that they couldn't wallow voluptuously in stocks and shares all week and break brush to grouse-shoot in the northern thicket on the weekend. So, it occurred to them that the really great thing would be to shoot driven game as Harold Macmillan did. Local boys were hired for the dangerous work. Children of members were forbidden as being a more valuable commodity than the native weed. Quinn and Stanton surreptitiously joined the line of beaters to drive the birds out of the swamps to the elegant sports waiting on high ground. Grouse began to fly in low trajectories before them. Sometimes they heard only the dense burr of wingbeat; more often the birds were visible too, brown and boreal, heavy on short blurred wings. There were more than twenty boys with pine boughs as switches, threshing rhythmically through the tugging underbrush and by now the birds were going off everywhere like bits of firecracker, buzzing, going off singly or in coveys and pairs but always forward toward the sports. The shooting started and the beaters got spattered with pellets. The younger boys sat down to cry. Stanton got stung on the face but kept going until he found the gunners. He gathered weapons; at first, by surprise and then at gunpoint.

But as time went by, the justice of his more extreme actions, though he retained his moral tone, became obscure. As a young man, the popularity of the "Gotcha" (derives from "Got you!") served to spotlight Stanton's virtues of nerve, craft and originality; such words, anyway, stood behind the deeds of that epoch in Stanton's life. During the archaic period, any dropping of one's pants in a public place under any circumstance qualified so long as the principal shouted "Gotcha!" to attract attention to the act. Later, the so-called Multiple Gotcha, commonly employing a speeding convertible, attracted the most approval. Then the "Press," which involved *pressing* the exposed buttocks to the rear window of a slow-moving vehicle was admired. Predictably, a point system sprang up, reputations were made and extenuating circumstances honored. "Throwing" a Gotcha while pursued by the police was a maneuver that brought one young competitor (Quinn) near permanent fame. Too, the nature of the victims sometimes necessitated a corresponding raising or lowering of point awards; thus, it was fair to expect a bonus increment for throwing an amazingly explicit or unexampled Gotcha at religious personnel. On the other hand, sly Gotchas, ones that were not forthright in any way, or ones directed at the very old or otherwise unalert, would frequently encounter a docking of points. Who were the competitors and who the judges? They were self-appointed; a moment's notice would do. Each competitor carried his own lifetime scorecard with a brief description of the play and, opposite, a point award initialed by the witnessing judge, usually another competitor, or "thrower." For example, an entry might read: *"Slow moon hangover shot from right front at nuns and children. 5 pts. v.s."* In this, the Gotcha (the exposed view of naked buttocks was known as "the moon") had been thrown at a slow rate of speed from a car, the behind actually appearing to hang out of the right front window, at a group of nuns and children. Simple? One more: *"Spread-eagle moon from back of reversing convertible directed from extreme close range at opera star Lucia Schifosa (screams). 20 pts. v.s."* Self-explanatory. A historical note is in order: this was the first of Quinn's competitive maneuvers in the New Year's *mano a mano* with Vernor Stanton; in this, the two young men acted as judges for one another (see Stanton's initials). In passing, it will be noticed that the term "moon" gradually came to be used as a verb; and indeed the whole process was finally called "mooning" and did not at all mean "to pass time in a listless manner" as the *Oxford English Dictionary* has it.

The New Year's *mano a mano* was never finished. Quinn led with the moon above. Stanton countered with a weak shot on foot at, in turn, a druggist, a young couple and a mounted policeman who lashed his horse in futile pursuit. Quinn confirmed his lead with a nice Standing Press against a restaurant window with a point-escalating Narrow Escape. Stanton's next shot restored the tie and in any other circumstance would have been match point: after a ten-minute delay during which they smoked nervously and silently, Stanton invited Quinn, now judge, back into the restaurant. They sat down unrecognized. Soup was ordered. An instant after it was served, Stanton was pointing from his position atop his chair at the hypothetical fly in the soup; his pants of course were around his ankles while he contrived by an imperceptible movement of his feet to present a "Full Moon," that is, a 360-degree view; needless to say, the "*dark side* of the moon" horrified the multitude!

The escape this time was so close that they were actually caught; and Stanton, whose position was somewhat worse, being pantless, got a bit of work with the nightstick. The policeman grunted "I hate an exhibitionist!" between the blows. They went to jail.

Quinn tried to think. This was all pouring through his mind very fast now. How much of it was getting to Janey? He tried, "Where was I?"

"You went to jail."

"Did I tell you how the jailbirds tried to initiate us?" Vernor had, she said. Quinn remembered Stanton as being invincible. The jailbirds made a practice of "stomping" sex offenders, which is what they were in the purblind eyes of the law. Quinn remembered Stanton, his shirt around him in strips like Captain Blood, the heavy fists snaking out and making clean resonant connections with chins. Like a sporty club fighter, his feet were light, shuffling, gripping only to set up a lead or a finishing shot. Stanton danced between the built-in benches, never bumping anyone or anything, just unleashing these long, snaky calamities. Afterward, there was peace, fingerpaints and byplay with the sheriff, Fredson W. Brown, the arresting officer who, after two weeks of heavy bribing, tried to get the book thrown at them anyway. With the fingerpaints, Stanton did a series of panels illustrating the sheriff committing unnatural acts upon livestock. The last panel purported to be a quote from Fredson Brown: "I *like* boys and girls," it said. "but a goat is numero uno." Quinn and Stanton were found guilty of indecent exposure. The sentence was commuted. They had records. Prints went to the FBI and both would forever afterward be suspects in any sex crime committed in their neighborhoods. Quinn had been interrogated six times, Stanton more often. Stanton was once grilled in connection with the rape and murder of an infant. A year afterward, he was tipped off that he would be questioned about his possible role in a pornography ring. A detective soon appeared camouflaged as a Southern racetrack tout in a Haspel drip-dry madras and summer straw. Working fast, Stanton had the complete works of Jane Austen rebound in separate volumes under the titles of *Lewd Awakening, Emma, Businessman's Lunch, She Let Him Continue* and *Persuasion*. The clever maneuver produced a false arrest; Stanton sued for harassment, collected a clean ten grand he didn't need and used it to start a wine cellar.

It would be hard to say how long after that, he and Quinn met in the D-Day Bar and Grill, a mock bunker filled with war materials, bombs painted to look like happy fishes, land mines, howitzers, portable field toilets. Stanton was still depressed about the interrogations, Quinn amused; amused, that is, until he got an idea of Stanton's ungodly depression. Stanton said that they were right, he deserved the worst. He had gotten some very convincing anonymous calls, one person calling him the "lowest form of human refuse." "And what is that?" Stanton had asked, his humor intact. He confessed they were getting to him. And Quinn could see he was in distress. It assumed the familiar atrabilious humor at the start ("Fuck the Magna Carta in the ass"). By the time they left the bar and headed for the D.A.C., Stanton's face had become a stone mask of thwarted rebellion. Quinn babbled at him and to him, from the heart and as best he could. They sat in the balcony over the pool, looking down at the empty green rectangle with its white water-polo backboards and undulant racing lanes. They swam and did cannonballs off the low board for which they were already too old. They went into the gym and Quinn got a basketball, dribbled preoccupied and did half-hearted lay-ups as Stanton bounced somberly on a nearby trampoline. They strolled naked except for medicated paper slippers and talked about the fathers-and-sons days they had attended, diving for silver dollars in the pool and afterward listening to Eddie Peabody in the auditorium. It was no use. Stanton's face remained pinched, a congestion of nerve ends. He challenged Quinn to a game of billiards and no more than got started before he slapped his cue stick across the table with a small cry and suggested dinner. Quinn watched him try to eat his way out of his depression. Consuming mechanically *tournedos de boeuf* and a thirty-dollar bottle of Château Margaux, he scribbled his number on the check and jumped up. Quinn went with him to the lobby where he bought a fistful of cigars and stuck them in his vest pocket. Out front he pressed a bill pointlessly into the doorman's hand and waited for his car to be brought. It was a winter night, black and cold to silence. When the car came, Stanton pressed another bill. "The thing is," he said to Quinn and stopped, something racing behind his eyes. He went around the driver's door. Quinn followed and said that it had been unfair to drag him around from one build-up to another and drive off. Stanton replied combatively from inside the car, "Well, that may be what I'll do, old pal . . ." and trailed off. He rested the bridge of his nose on the steering wheel and said, "It's nothing. I'm boxed in, is all. Nothing." He sat up and drove away. The next time Quinn saw him was a few weeks ago, standing in his linen shorts, sweat runneling off him: the heroic manner.

Interim reports, less somber than expected, suggested furious play, operating out of his boat down South. Quinn had a letter describing tarpon fishing at Big Pine Key, Florida. Then a newspaper article from Key West: Stanton and friends had stormed the naval installation there; on capture, they had tried to pass themselves off as Castro partisans. For a while, cards and letters: gambling at Grand Bahama, pig shooting at Abaco, tarpon again at Andros, whoring at Nassau, partying at Eleuthera. On Grand Turk Island he was persuaded to put up twenty thousand dollars to investigate the possibility of celestial navigation in sea turtles. News of him began to abate in the Antilles proper. He was charged with espionage in Haiti quite arbitrarily and he was convinced by the Tonton Macoute that it would be clever to fly out and leave the boat. He bought another from an English yacht broker in Antigua and wrote Quinn to tell him he was going to Puerto Rico because of his love for *beisbol*. Quinn didn't hear from him again. Throughout these letters, though he had little to go on, Quinn got an impression of metallic insensibility that approached stupefaction, like letters from someone in shell shock. The rest was from Janey on; and she, it seemed, wasn't talking. "Are you?"

"Nope."

"Why not?"

"Because there is no place to start. It doesn't make a story." A single strangely shaped shadow revealed the declivity of her cheek and any motion at all made her eyes go from reflecting to bottomless. No wonder she had Stanton under such crazy control as Quinn was now sure she had, dancing like a circus horse, a little out of hand perhaps, but out there on the lead under unreckonable command. Quinn liked this thought: Stanton a little dappled stallion waltzing on a barrel head, jumping through pastel flames; behind, the gallery in regular ascending semicircles of vacuous faces; Stanton's hoofs muffled in the sawdust as he trots steadily round Janey in silk top hat and tails, her whip curling toward his dappled buttocks like a silk thread. Then, after the last hoop, Stanton fetches up under the big top; there is mechanical applause like seawaves. A tiny car drives up and skids to a stop. Enthusiastic applause as a family of midgets bails out with luggage. The pony begins to go sour. He whinnies aggressively. The midgets stop in trepidation. The booing begins like the groaning of a tree about to fall and rises as the pony rushes among the midgets, striking out with varnished crescent hoofs, the booing rising as the midgets begin to take a beating; then the inscrutable crowd comes out of the bleachers and smothers the pony in sharp downward blows like the branches of a collapsing tree. As it came to Quinn's mind, he wondered if it was accurate.

Janey said: "One night, in Puerto Rico, Vernor heard a woman crying on the balcony outside his hotel. He went out and saw her leaning against the wall covering her face up with her hands. She was still crying. Vernor asked what happened and she said she had been attacked by a man. Vernor asked her what he looked like and she took her hands down from her face. Vernor asked her what he looked like again and she stared at him just a minute and said, 'You.'" The woman, Janey said, was her Aunt Judy. Vernor was horrified and fascinated, he fell in love. But she only went out with him and let him stay with her betweentimes: there were others. "I had to console the poor lovesick baby and, oh, me, he was starry-eyed! He offered her the world and everything he had. Now, then, one day he came over in the morning. I think it was on a hunch. Judy was sleeping in the bedroom with a dealer from the El Convento. And Vernor smoked and fussed and tried to talk to me. I can tell you it was tense, boy. I talked my head off. Vernor was puffing his cigarette and squinting at the bedroom door until Judy came out in a peignoir still beautiful but very rundown looking and in a bad mood. Vernor tried too hard to be pleasant and told her she looked mussed up or something, though maybe it was only the unfortunate lighting. Judy said, 'I just woke up. Get it? I just woke up.' He began yelling that someone was there. The dealer walked out of the bedroom, fully dressed and said, 'A for excellent.' He had a pistol in his hand and he wasn't waving it around or anything. He just had it. He walked right past Vernor and went over to the mirror and tucked the pistol under his chin and smoothed his hair down with both hands. Then he put the pistol in the top of his pants and squeezed the knot of his tie between his thumbs and put the pistol in his pocket. He asked Vernor how he looked and Vernor said he looked as sharp as a tack. And then the dealer asked how he liked the tie and I thought somebody would get killed but Vernor said that the tie was of the very finest." Later, Stanton befriended the dealer and took him deep-sea fishing and by some slip or concatenation of circumstances left the dealer in a yellow rubber raft a hundred miles off the Mayaguana Bank.

When the police informed Stanton that though the dealer would not let them bring him to justice, they thought he ought to know the man was in the hospital with third degree burns from the sun. "Next time," Stanton said, "he won't leave his Coppertone on his beach blanket." Judy used the police without reserve; she kept a small, gray one at her door with instructions to shoot or arrest Stanton on sight. "He got so desperate he settled for me," said Janey. "And I couldn't pass him up."

Quinn helped her with her coat. It was a dressy, tailored coat with a velvet collar and looked good with the old cotton slacks she wore. Quinn could see that she was feeling what had settled over the club; the apprehension widened her eyes and emphasized the almost foxlike shape of her face. Then his mind wandered from Janey in dejection and replaced her with Mary Beth complete with bagpipes. Doggedly, Quinn watched himself unwind her kilt; but instead of the herring-white Scots flesh he has resigned himself to, he discovers a set of prickly duck-hunters' underwear. What's the meaning of this?

"The meaning of what?"

"Talking to myself."

What a smell! Anyone would think that people who had as many pretenses as these club members had would have the decency to go a little way from the tent. And the body odor, especially the women, was not the reassuring funk of laborers; this was the smell of people who had been deep in deodorants until a couple of days ago; it was something smarmy, acidic and sour. Quinn made his way along the tent. He recoiled from one odor to another until, in resignation, he accepted and his nose pumped steadily at the single generalized odor that was a meld of everything from axilla to organic debris and smelled like clam soil.

People went to and fro as though in a blackout, with a rather useless air of carrying on. A portable generator ran somewhere and lightbulbs hung in the trees, swung and heaved in the breeze and threw monstrous shadows everywhere. The children were playing in the black rectangle of shadow at the end of the tent and their fierce voices came brokenly. ". . . no, you can't! . . . Eat it raw!" Then the piping voice of a little girl, "Okay for you, Billy! Now I have to kick you in the noogies!" Quinn was shoved rudely from behind. It was Fortescue carrying the front end of a small platform. "If you can't help, get out of the way." Stanton came past carrying the other end. They placed it opposite the center of the collapsed tent, that is, between the tent and the Bug House. Quinn glared after Fortescue. When Fortescue had put his end down he looked back and caught Quinn's eye. "Go home, Quinn! Please go!"

"Let's hurry it up," Stanton said to him. "I've got stuff to do."

"Is this speech going to be long?" Fortescue asked.

"Brief, very brief, very brief."

"What about a little fireworks first?"

"Okay, give 'em fireworks."

"The singing though."

"Give 'em the fucking singing."

"What about a couple of rockets, see, and then you

have the singing coming right in there afterward."

"Get this: I don't care. But whatever it is, make it snappy."

"Sure, okay. We have all the time in the world. Spengler burned his chronicle, you know. So, we'll have more time for you."

Quinn approached. "What'd he burn his chronicle for?"

"Come on," Fortescue said, "get a move on."

"Said we don't deserve it," Stanton said impatiently.

"Everybody together for the fireworks and singing," Fortescue called. "Charles," he shouted past Quinn, "Reveille!" Charles Murray materialized looking a little worn but well preserved. He put the bugle to his mouth and took it down again.

"This won't be terribly good," he said.

"Blow," said Fortescue, and Murray raised the bugle to his smiling lips. What came out was nothing like Reveille at all. It was a forlorn sound and reminded Quinn of the noise that must have been made by those animals that were the transitional phase between birds and reptiles. But everyone gathered around and sat crosslegged in front of the platform, behind which Murray now knelt on one knee striking matches. Soon a little string of sparks hung in the air before him and he whirled, ran, then bit the dust as the first rocket, then the second and third shot aloft and burst flowers of color on the sky. Murray sang:

> "O-oh, say can you see,
> By the dawn's early light,
> What so proudly we hail," etc.

People took the song up, standing at attention under trees, canvas and the influence of intoxicants. Children ceased their industrious grubbing to salute our flag. When the singing stopped, more rockets went aloft. One fell over as it was lit and hit Mrs. Scott in the belly without damage. The projectile was covered with a blanket before it went off and when it did, it did so with a cough and writhed like an animal underneath, finally burning its way through in a thousand places. Mrs. Scott, meanwhile, ran through the camp howling. Quinn remarked the quality of her voice which was like the singing tops of his youth: a fluty, metallic sound, cyclical and, for a human voice, quite unacceptable. Stanton cried, "Shut the twat up before she wrecks the party!" This swung unfriendly attention upon himself that was only dissipated by the spectacle of a fiery wheel racing on a guy wire, back and forth between two trees. Then Quinn watched Scott confront Stanton and tell him he didn't have to put up with this kind of behavior. "Do you realize what could have happened to her?" exclaimed the irate academician. "That could have blown her insides out!"

"No harm there."

"*What—?*"

Stanton walked away. The attention of the crowd now flickered between him and the fireworks and their eyes seethed like frogs' eggs about to hatch. Stanton prowled. When there was a pause in the fireworks, he cried, "ON WITH THE GIZMOS!" Stars and stripes appeared, pinwheels and carnations popped on the sky like drops of paint on glass. One rocket went up and exploded with a terrific crack, and since there was no visible display the darkness seemed a picture. Murray ran around with a lighted punk setting things off, rockets that shot from troughs or off sticks, some that whistled and screamed like V-2s and buzz bombs. What was needed was the sound of hordes, real Dino di Laurentiis hordes, Kirk Douglas directing Vandals, Saxons, Celts, Wogs, their women in tailored skins showing a bit of tit. Murray did his best. He raced around setting fire, but it was so incomplete without the sound of hordes, though the steady upward stream of fiery trails, the streaking back and forth of the burning wheel, the whistles, explosions and chemical colors aloft were enough. "ON WITH THE GIZMOS!" At the far end of the tent, the children were lofting firecrackers into the group, and when they'd blow and the bits of fiery cardboard flew around, the women screamed and struck at their clothes as though there were spiders on them.

"How about lending a hand for a change," Fortescue said to Quinn, indicating the antic Murray.

"Right you are," Quinn said, not moving but winking most agreeably. Quinn went into the tent to get away from the fun. The first thing he noticed were the shapes that the lights threw on the tent from outside, distorted human shapes that moved at unnatural speed, appeared as recognizable silhouettes, then burst out of their forms to blacken the whole end of the improvised tent. Under the canvas ledge, reading a magazine, was the handsome little mother who had caused Quinn to fall down so foolishly at the beach. He wandered toward her as though on a retracting tether, as though he needn't even move his feet. She put the magazine down and smiled first on one side and then on the other. When he spoke, his voice came from the past. "Nice to see you," he said, after Scott. She wouldn't pretend to speak. She smiled now and then arbitrarily and had very white teeth, very white. "I've b·en·thinking about you ever since," Quinn said. He sat down and began to poke and fuss around experimentally. Half an hour later, giddy with foreplay, he thinks, Oh, my god, my god, oh, my god. Can they see me? Quinn looked around to the entire open front of the tent. Oh, my god, I know they could if they wanted to and I don't care I'm going at it anyway and isn't she nice. He could see the line of the bathing suit that had confined his view at the beach while her child beat the sand with its little shovel. My god, I am going to score right out of the blue, I am I tell you. Spengler, someone, keep them distracted, tell them this proves it, the West is not declining, or does this prove it is; but give them absolutely any theory that will distract them and I will score if you do; keep them mindful of our country's origins. The rockets' red glare. Let them have it. Quinn worked toward the last buttons one-handed; the other did its rooting with an especially scurvy lewd-ness; she rested on her elbows and the breasts slipped to the sides, then she let down on her back. In a minute I'll be at it like some hyperthyroid mongoose. She hooked a forefinger in the corner of her pretty mouth, her face rosy with the strange light, the monster show still sweep-ing over the canvas from outside. Isn't she lovely. Like some precocious baby, my valentine goo goo. He began to thrash and struggle violently with his own clothes like a pickerel in a bucket. Get these god damned duds off without losing the old momentum. Keep it up someone out there but I don't care if you don't. Nothing is to come between me and my febrile plans. Now shall I introduce myself? She doesn't smell as bad as some of these birds. The bombs bursting in air gave proof through the night that our flag was still there. There: look at me, naked and glorious, God is a good god in his fashion. That's it, take the little devil, he's yours. The forefinger still in the mouth. Then she puts the thumb in the other corner and neatly collapses her face by removing a surprising set of dentures. Ohmygod! Her chin is under that nose. That face is trying to smile. That face thinks this is funny. I don't care I don't care. Put a bag and remember the flesh of this flesh. Presently she accommodates him, as a wild Cucaracha howls outside on the loudspeaker. She stares listlessly at a small spot on the canvas. Quinn lost no time. As he did so, he heard a cry, "ON WITH THE GIZMOS!" then perceived waggish Stanton, winking, taking a chorus of La Cucaracha and doing an expert Samba in the entranceway. Quinn, expended, could hardly go on. He was now irritable and —he faced up to it—doing little more than lurching. "Keep it upp," she gummed impassively. Quinn knew that people had been watching by now and he was upset. "They've seen my ass!" he whispered harshly.

"I don't care I don't care. Keep it upp."

"But I can't get going!" He was now outright cranky. She looked at him. Her eye, grave and considerable in its fixity, caught his: venom. She got up and tipped him over.

"Some gwatitude!"

She began to dress, Quinn too. Outside Stanton had begun haranguing informally. Quinn went to the entrance, then turned back. "Why did you let me walk in like that and . . ." Her jaw worked as she sorted out her clothes. She didn't bother to look up at his struggle for words. The teeth beside her seemed to have a bleak life of their own and rested on the ground in mechanical hilarity.

"What'th the diff, anyway?"

"A big difference to me!"

"Aw, poopoo, you want to be loffed. Ith that it?"

"Yes!" he said indignantly. When she didn't actually have her chin pressed under her nose, she managed to retain a woebegone beauty, as if an aging of her former, toothed self. "I want just that." Quinn got up without a word and went outside. Something was delaying Stanton. Quinn could see Janey nearby, aloof, and hauntingly disconnected from the heated talk around her. Stanton was disagreeing about something and as Quinn wandered toward him, he saw the young woman he had just left talking gaily with a companion and pointing at him. The extinction of decency. She hadn't troubled to replace her teeth. Even from here Quinn noted the way her slack lips tugged around her mobile tongue when she talked. Stanton was now quarreling behind him and he wanted to avoid it. In the good warm night the sounds of other fireworks from afar were like war: towns going under, divisions, heavy stuff being moved. Before him the tent heaped up white in the light like meringue. Was this really so bad? He felt very even right now and did not believe in decline. He attributed the feeling to having been able to take his pleasure like an animal. That face he didn't want to see gazing at a spot upon the canvas, the dewy, girlish flesh presented as foursquare as a billboard: just fine, just what was required to keep the spirit intact.

Janet Fortescue walked past, giving him a little wave. She was too heavy in the leg, almost grossly so, and sought to counter it by affecting a startling lightness of head and torso, delicate, floating gestures, gay tossings of the head. It was a little like movies of man's first hapless attempts at flight when the sodden earth and its gravity were shown to dominate the frailest constructs of wood and lacquered cloth. Her hands fluttered an abandoned greeting to Murray as he labored over a rocket trough; she ran past him like a rhino. He took off after her on wild flapping feet.

"Come on," Fortescue said, "you've got to be good for something. Talk Stanton into letting us dig up the time capsule before he makes his speech." Quinn marveled at the power and leverage Stanton had acquired.

"I can't talk him into anything."

"What *can* you do? What can you do?"

"Beastly little. My proudest accomplishment is of being no use to you." Fortescue ambled away, organizing, saying, *"The dead weight I have known!"*

Dilemmas: Quinn was bored with marshaling and being marshaled; it was how he made his living. For the time being, he preferred, as a spectator, fixed ideas and compulsion: they were picturesque. Stanton's playing every man for a fool was, right now, fine with Quinn.

And this was just the situation for him to perform freely in. The usual rules seemed to have expired. Except for a few holdouts, mostly the kind of men who get more and more dolled up the more uncivilized things become and who now stood around the fire sipping from Martini glasses in spurious gentility, except for these, it could have been the Bronze Age.

On the other hand, maybe it would be exactly this that would constrain Stanton. Heretofore he had relied heavily on the expectations of others for his effects. And when he didn't find them, he could become dangerously ill-humored. Quitting the only job he had ever had, for example, he had relieved himself in a potted plant in the crowded executives' lounge. To his great amusement and gratification, many looked with horror at him over their coffee cups. Then his boss, in destructive civility, called from his own crowded table, "Mine's bigger than yours, Vernor!" And Stanton went unexpectedly surly and had to be turned out by the police. Since he owned the company, no charges were pressed. Was something of this obtaining now? The closer the club moved toward a state of which he would have been expected to approve, the more humorless he became in his stunts. But, from what Janey had to say, the process had begun much earlier.

Someone convinced Stanton to wait until after the time capsule, and the group around him broke up. Everyone began to move toward the flagpole and Fortescue pawed his way through the crowd until he was in front. Quinn, who was no longer the same, skipped alongside him and cried, "Can I dig? Let me dig! I get to dig!"

Fortescue stretched out his arms to stop the crowd, fetched a good, ash-handled shovel from the tent and pressed it on him like a rifle, telling him to be his guest. Until now, Quinn had enjoyed their friction but this hostile flattening of the lips he observed now and the closing of wrinkled flesh around diamantine and wicked eyes was something new. Stanton came up, exasperated and happy all at once. "You're the court digger, is it?" he said. "Well, that's splendid. Keep the dirty work in the family; and remember this, that you are never so human as when you're digging a hole." On close examination, Stanton was quite battered. Most striking was the forefinger of his right hand which was like a radish with swelling. He walked along turning the shovel blade in front of his view, admiring its brightness, the cleanliness of its concave shape, and feeling the murmurous swell of crowd behind him.

"I saw Olive," Stanton said.

"What did Olive say to you?"

"He threw me out," Stanton grinned, "for conduct unbecoming a gentleman. He said if I ever returned he would deal with me. I will return tonight at the head of a phalanx of buffoons. See, Olive got the drop on me, for I had become drowsy with my amours. It was pretty spooky too, boy. And I do fear that if it hadn't been for the dramatically satisfactory pleas of my little piece out there in the bush that Olive would have seen to my ventilation. As it was, he thrashed me with a stick." Quinn knew instinctively and with resentment that the little piece was Lu. They stopped at the shallow crater. The flagpole lay uprooted, with a ragged circle of concrete clinging to its base. The pole took the light of their lanterns and made a tapering streak outward into the darkness where Olive hid. Quinn stepped in, bending and taking up a handful of sandy loam. "Straight down?" he called.

"Straight down!" they all answered. He could smell the moist soil and severed roots. He got a sight of Fortescue and bent to his work, stepping on the shovel and slipping the bright blade into the earth; then his hands at the end of the handle, he tipped up the load, slid his left hand to the head of the shovel, called, "All clear?" and threw the load in Fortescue's face.

They grappled. Quinn allowed Fortescue to strangle him a little before saying, "I prithee, take thy fingers from my throat for, though I am not splenetive and rash yet have I in me *something dangerous!*" He threw the hands away, rising up, fomenting in mockturtle rage. Others jumped into the pit to separate them. "Gentlemen—!"

Quinn continued, "Why, I will fight with him upon this theme until my eyelids no longer wag!" They dragged Fortescue out of the hole, pretending to minister to him.

"There is no dealing with that Quinn," said Stanton. "Under his Age of Eisenhower exterior is a mindless beast that will stop at nothing." In Stanton's voice was a single dominant tone: victory. Quinn, he believed, was backsliding.

"And you?" Quinn asked, deep in the misunderstanding stares of the club.

"The reverse," Stanton threw off. "A mindless beast

with an Age of Eisenhower interior. It makes a disappointing combination." Quinn began to dig, wondering which of these varieties would admit of sanity. The bright blade scooped through sand and into light gravel and then light clay that let him step up with both feet onto the shovel and sink slowly and cleanly to earth. He grunted at the far end, feeling the powerful flexing of the ash handle in his palms as a heavy wedge of smooth clay lifted from the hole. He worked hard and made a square clean-sided shaft in the ground that went deeper and deeper. He took off his shirt and felt the sweat run off him in rivulets despite the night air. The lanterns were above him in a row like ships' lights and above the lanterns the faces gazed down with an intense pallor like shamans' masks. He knew that his muscles were engorged and would be gleaming attractively in their multifold bevelings. The toothless wonder must be up there gumming in lust for this shoveling master man.

All of them heard the shovel ring out. Quinn felt around with its blade: a hard curved surface like a boulder. He took his time, sighting and sizing. He crouched down in the pit and began to scrabble in the confined space, clawing the dirt out around the object. Stones ran back in, aggravating him, and he worked double time to keep ahead of them, finally getting his hands underneath and slowly heaving its weight. His chin strained upward against the tendons of his neck and his navel felt as though it were dilating and would momentarily extrude forty feet of intestine. He heaved the thing out and lights played over its surface. It was a boulder. Quinn waited to catch his breath. He listened for words of sympathy but heard only the waiting silence of the club above him. He touched the shovel to the bottom again, the delicate sacklike bottom any hole has, pushed through it a little with his foot and found the time capsule resting as it had for one century. It was light, a small strongbox, and he climbed out of the hole carrying it, examining it: it was oblong with something very much like asphalt or tar covering it. A lock, thick with verdigris, hung from an ornate hasp. "The way I look at it—" Fortescue was heard to begin, "*some*body—" Quinn moved into the light and the people moved with him. "The way *I*—"

"Who's got the key?" Quinn asked. Everyone laughed and Quinn did too, as though he had been joking. He was convinced enough of what the club had always prated about its continuity to think that the key would have been handed on. He set the box on its end and whanged the lock off with the shovel. "My own view would be—" Fortescue pressed. "Oh." He finished, seeing Quinn open it slowly as the lid lifted stiffly on its hinges. The inside of the box was japanned metal. A large rolled sheet of some paper or parchment comprised its sole contents. This was tied about with ribbon that rubbed away to dust under Quinn's finger. He unrolled what proved to be a huge photograph and pinned its corners with stones and joined the press of heads bent beneath the naphtha lantern and studied it as long as his stunned brain would permit and sat back with a gasp. The others were erect, out of the light. All the sounds of the night stood out around their silence. Stanton's voice emerged from behind, rigorously suppressed but thick with joy. "Don't let a little thing like this spoil our party, er, ON WITH THE GIZMOS!"

Quinn had to admit, and not unruefully, that Stanton had the goods on them. The picture was so fantastic, yet so personal a jest from a century ago that suddenly the place did seem to have history, a history that would require denial if these people were to go on in the old way. Surely the question on top of the photograph blaring in gold leaf *Dearest Children of the Twentieth Century, Do You Take Such Pleasures as Your Ancestors?* could not be answered so forthrightly as it was asked. Surely nothing they could say or do now would flail the eye as this rickety nineteenth century light with which the photographer had recorded so outlandish a sexual circus at full progress. The artifice of obvious poses hardly tempered the fact that every postural permutation and every phase of the spectrum of perversion from fellatio and cunnilingus to sodomy was portrayed. The picture was a rash of the most blatant buggery, among other things, with one distinguished-looking gentleman assaulting a patient Irish setter. Laced through the picture, the younger people including Quinn's great-grandmother, copulated shyly or abashedly wagged and spread. Exhibitionists and masturbators crowded forward without concealing the Bug House whose screens obscured human contents and made of them vague and suggestive blobs. If anything, the picture had retained a bucolic quality of leaf-dappling light upon mound after mound of gently contorted flesh. Only the bits of mockingly retained clothing—one sodomist wore a derby—reminded you that this was the last century; that and the strange and precise light. Each vignette, if the whole could be so divided, was signed in the unique hands of that era. Quinn wondered what impulse had united these people now scattered through various respectable graveyards in so preposterous an act. But it was impossible to make an imaginary reconstruction. The fact of the photograph and the world it revealed now held an adamant reality that was at once as radiant and cloudy as myth.

They walked as penitents, each, it is certain, with the same picture in mind. Stanton stepped onto the dais. The faithful gathered crosslegged before him. Stanton had the photograph. "Charles," he said, turning into the dark behind him. "Charles, what about a gizmo or two?" A half-dozen rockets streamed up behind him and burst upon the sky, their dream colors rinsing down the night in fading pastel tracks. "Thank you, Charles, for your rockets, for your gizmos and for just being you."

"Go to hell, Stanton," he said quietly and urbanely. "would you do that?"

"I appreciate your suggestions and will try my uttermost to follow them. Now find yourself a place in the peanut gallery and try to relax. This is no clambake. You are among friends who worship the air you walk on." A snore of ugly laughter arose as Murray sat down. Quinn picked up a handful of the loose garbage that decorated the ground and slung it at Stanton. "Go back where you came from!" he heckled. "It's a bum act!"

"Okay, old pal," said Stanton softly, then went on with his address. "My dearly beloved in Christ, I don't mean to rub anyone's nose in what should be thrust from us in indignation; but I have before me a filthy, *filthy*, foul and lubricious photograph which I am only too afraid throws a rather startling light on the history of this old and once venerable club—"

Fortescue: "It's a fraud and a lie!" Fortescue had a lot riding on this. He yelled as though he would go for broke. "A cheat! A chee-e-et!"

Stanton asked, "Well? Boys and girls? Is it? A cheat?" Perplexity, negative murmurs answered him. Quinn believed the photograph was genuine. "The answer is, it is not a cheat. No, it is, I'm afraid, something else again. Whew! It's a bit hard to get it into my head that this swinish pack of human refuse from which we all descend has put an end to our little organization by remote control. The end, the end. Finished. Extinction as in dinosaurs, top hats, the great auk—"

"Prove it, you bugger!" snapped the wife of a former Secretary of Defense.

"—the Carolina parakeet, the Everglades kite, the ivory-billed woodpecker, the narwhal. Kiddies, the experiment fails. A hundred years trying to make a single silk purse out of a few hundred sows' ears went for nothing. My dearly beloved in Yazoo, who were we trying to kid?" Stanton continued to speak on the dais but now inaudible as though he were speaking to himself as he might well have been. He murmured away about its being a barnyard and of his being no better than a forlorn peahen divvying up the chickenfeed with the rest of the animals. All around him the club was somehow at bay, though Quinn could see they wouldn't listen to Stanton much longer. Stanton implored them to join their country in praying for the bomb it so richly deserved and insisted that vaporization was no barrier in the empire of love, the shining city. "Cherish my molecules as myself," he demanded; rather seriously off his rocker, Quinn thought. "I intend to be striding the heavenly blast under the reliable auspices of the great Numero Uno in the sky by six A.M. Greenwich time."

Fortescue gained the dais saying they had had a snootful of speaking in tongues. His face was elongated with rage, the thin Puritan lips like the slit of a razor. "Need I remind you," he intoned soberly, "that we are at war?" A woeful Andean groan passed over the crowd. No one moved. The hot night seemed to have produced a languor and the meridional temperament had otherwise made gains. The fact was that the group lay around fondling one another, absently as though the photograph had shown them historical duties and an immediate future. Stanton and Fortescue were the only warriors in camp; Quinn was an outsider of some kind; detumescence alone made him that.

Fortescue's eyes swam with light as they welled with tears. "I intend to go, with you—" he paused a very long time and looked around him, as perfectly tincan a little demagogue as possible "—or without you. And I pray God—" another infuriating pause "—that there may be men among you." He swiveled, eyes spilling, off the platform, hitched his rifle onto his shoulder and headed into the darkness. Quinn, who thought himself unaffected, wanted to give him the finger. "Come on chirruns," implored Stanton. "Close de ranks!" They leered at him. Suddenly, he was among them, wading into the first row. "By the light of burning martyrs," he cried, "let's make our cause live!" Then they began to stir and were in their places, a single tissue, only a moment longer. It broke: Scott's wife arose and bolted only to be tackled by an old gentleman who bit her leg while she squealed and the antiquarian himself thrashed the both of them with a switch, giggling and rubbing himself. "We're coming!" they cried. "We'll join you! We'll go anywhere! The whites of their eyes and our flag was still there." Mere dissembling promises, hardly the thing for an army. They drifted away like Indians into the darkness, squealing and trumpeting. Quinn watched smugly, only a short time before feeling his irony melt off its stick and splatter at his feet: he got up and began to hunt his friend from the tent. Stanton had Janey by the arm and was trying to take her on the manhunt. "Vernor," she repeated giddily, "I'm silly putty in your hands." Quinn went hopefully to the tent, then stopped. It sounded like a hog pen; but so fierce and authentic that he for a moment didn't dare approach; when he did, he went forward to see what manner of heroes were these who braved such a maniacal darkness. From the doorway, the bodies seemed to form a writhing false floor amid which it was impossible to isolate individuals. But near the door, Charles Murray and Janet Fortescue rolled about as Janet yelled, "Make it stand! Make it stand up!" Murray spotted Quinn and took off after him. This was exactly the thing to snap Quinn's overtasked mind and he ran for his life. He looked over his shoulder and saw Murray gaining on him with a crazy windmilling of limbs and giddy squealing. Quinn whirled at bay, then caught him by the shirt and held him off. "Charles! Cut it out!" Murray's lips trumpeted toward Quinn. He was vamping him.

"I kees you all ovair!"

Quinn cuffed him sharply but not unkindly and said there would be no action. "What's the use?" said Murray, wiping his mouth with the back of his hand.

"I admit your opportunities look reduced. But maybe if you moved around in the dark . . ."

"Yes, all right. I wonder if you could look after Janet."

"I'll try. If I can't, I'll find someone." Quinn thought of the Irish setter.

"Appreciate it. Welp, I better get started." Quinn watched him slip away, already regaining his hysterical bounce as he disappeared, leaving Quinn alone in his own humming lull wondering what had happened not only to this crowd of trusty bourgeoises but to himself that he could go back for seconds on the toothless wonder or a stride or two later advise Murray to try to knock something off in the dark. "Golly," he thought, "the moral dubiousness of it!"

He completely forgot Janet Fortescue until he crossed back into the lighted center of the compound and saw her on the dais with a megaphone singing.

> *Goan a take*
> *a sen a men*
> *ull jerny,*
> *Goan a take*
> *a trip for love.*

Such a grotesquery, normally tolerable or amusing to him, tonight was a crucifixion. A moment later, he was beside her taking choruses. Cheek to cheek, they barked their lyrics at the chromium ring on the small end of the megaphone.

> *Seven!*
> *That's the time*
> *we'll meet*
> *at seven . . .*

When they finished, they faced each other, holding hands. She was wearing a Pendleton shirt and khakis. Quinn saw where one of the belt loops was distended from the weight of her slide rule. "Take me with you," she said. Quinn thought that when she wasn't singing she had a beautiful voice.

"No can do."

"Why, baby? Prior commitments?"

"That's the one," said Quinn. She sighed.

"Well, the song is over—"

"—but the memory lingers on."

Quinn was away now, sailing across the green, green compound, away from the bug and bat whirling core of light that revealed Janet waving, "Bye, bye . . ."

"Ta ta," Quinn said, faking the tone. He was *in extremis.*

Why did I say that? Is something going on? He expected to come over the crest of the hill to find the moon smeared all over the earth, the color of milk of magnesia but thick as latex, moving and spreading its

anarchic power. And he thought, if I could leap into the
sky. If I could have ridden that horse skeleton into the
sky. If wishes were horses. If all the pieces were a whole.
If I could fly into the sky and watch through a spyglass:
they're warring now, now there's peace, now anarchy,
vengeances are loosed, plagues are loosed, flies are loosed
and Quinn is away sailing across green into green, his
green peeling from its green inside and I must have
freedom and it is only that which will do. The swamps
breed discontent and therefore bomb all moist places.
Wendell Willkie and the clear plastic tears of Mexican
virgins implore you to sink giggling beneath consideration until all the beasts of the zodiac raid your poor
brain. Remember that help yourself is a novel of please
and that if you try too hard you will be seen to the door,
your mind belly up and your hat in your hand. Life is
a greedy railroad and that's an end on it. What is the
future of man and his religions when scientists in a top-
secret laboratory have already constructed the first hydraulic nun? And which came first, the four-minute mile
or the three-minute egg? What is the principle of selec-
tive bungling? How is it practiced? Quinn could no more
answer than he could picture his own unconcern as he
sat in this cool woodland listening to the honking and
fluting of the unbridled lust of bankers and merchants.
It was this, he thought: it was postcoital depression at
institutional rates; it was a note from the world of excess;
it was the dejected piping of a *bourgeois gentilhomme;*
it was the squeal of the ultima fool, the whimper of a
magician with a trick knee; it was the bassoon section
of a downhill parade all the way from lower left to the

middle distance; men without views, true colors, bulk ambitions and high-speed dreams.

Each time Quinn, a kind of ghoul, sent up one of the rockets, he heard the roar of the horde from the woods toward the lake. By all signs, he was alone in the clearing. The sniveling, honking, fluting and licentious whimpering had stopped. The unmistakable odor of the fluids which excitation brings to the fore had blown away with the breeze of the North Woods and Quinn smelled only that breeze and the agreeable spice of burning rocket fuse. Another went up and showered pistachio green. The roar of the horde followed. Quinn liked this feeling of remote control. Another aloft and this one is . . . *Pock!* this one will just be the plain red. (Horde roars.) Now a multicolor followed by the straight exploder that you think leaves black light. A dimmer horde roaring. Quinn lights everything in sight and it is like D-Day. There is no response from the horde.

Quinn circled the high ground, keeping on the far edge of this elevated contour, toward the lake. When he reached the point of its perimeter that was closest to the lake, he could see them below. The illusion was of something under water which made light. You could see a shape of light moving in the trees as through the broken surface of water, and the shape was a marine one, enlarged at one end and tapering like a shark. The light was yellow with a patina of white. It all moved with the muttering of a horde toward the lake bed.

By traveling the downgrading edge of the ridge, Quinn was able to crosscut ahead of them and wait on the hard bed of the lake. He heard them approach now with a steady drone of voice that seemed pitched at some unnerving harmony and was punctuated with the regular tambourine crash of guns and equipment. The nearer they came, the more nervous it made Quinn, and in a moment he was back up on the slope of the ridge watching their progress below. As they came through the last trees at the edge of the lake bed, the broken sheen of lights appeared to be a swarm of fireflies. But when they moved into the open the light solidified into the single slender tapering shape again that undulated gently onto the floor of the lake.

Quinn was filled with horror. He watched their progress. When they reached the far end of the lake, the light closed in upon itself to form a ball and stayed that way for ten minutes throbbing very slightly in the blackness. When it moved off into the trees to become a swarm again and disappear, it left a single still light behind. Quinn headed for it in trepidation.

The expanse of the dry lake seemed endless and the thousands of fissures made his progress slow. As he approached the light, a darker shape like a huge blurred potato stood out beside it. He was hard put to distinguish it though, even standing before it. "*Shit fire!*" it said unconvincingly. It was Fortescue. He had been tarred and feathered. When Quinn asked, he said the Olives had gotten him. Fortescue sobbed and Quinn stared at him helplessly. The lamp threw a merciless light over him and he was unquestionably out for the duration. He was so heavily covered with tar that his limbs were indistinguishable; and out of the tar protruded a hundred thousand feathers, each with its own blue shadow. Fortescue's eyes were barbarically fierce spots in the roughly fledged surface. And when he opened his mouth to talk, the unreflecting contrast of feathers made his tongue and the inside of his mouth gleam unnaturally red as though poor Fortescue had been interrupted feeding on a corpse.

"Can you move?" Before he answered, the horde roared out louder than before for a long sustained moment and died away. "Can you walk?"

"No, God damn it, no. Give me a hand though and see if I can stand." Quinn took his thick roadlike arm and helped him to his feet. He stood in a stoop like a tremendous chicken and fell down again. "They laughed at me!" he bawled.

"Well, you look funny you know—" Fortescue began to pull himself together abruptly.

"Oh, but God damn it, Quinn, I'm going to die, it's so hot in here. I can't close my hands. If I blink, my whole scalp moves. I—" He began to cry slightly, then, with a heavy lateral movement, lurched over onto his stomach and sobbed like a child. Quinn felt tears start sympathetically to his own eyes and he laid his hand upon Fortescue's back. The heavy, feathered surface flexed very slightly from the heaving underneath.

"Did Earl do this to you himself?"

"Yes." A huge broken sigh expired. "But I don't blame him. None of this could have been thought up without Stanton."

"You really blame him for all this—"

"Certainly I do. Here I am crying in front of you. I don't suppose . . . I mean you'd never . . ."

"Not a word."

"These people have gone haywire tonight."

"I think so."

"The world isn't like this, is it?"

"I think it is."

"But Quinn, I'm an old man. It isn't like this."

"Yes, but I think it is." By this time, Quinn could see the light of the horde. It moved across the end of the lake toward the river. Once he had made certain that Fortescue would be all right and secure beside the lantern, he headed to intercept them.

At a long clearing in the birches, he found them preparing to duel. They were counting already. Olive moved a step at a time with exact placement of foot while Stanton goose-stepped in mockery. The horde stood back and Quinn crowded in with them where he was assured of what he had already known: lead bullets. Quinn felt a complete and hopeless quietude, as though it were a natural phenomenon. He couldn't resent what was happening because there was nothing for it, nothing; no flying tackles, nor interferences of authority, nor breakdowns, redemptions or recognitions; no dreams, plasma or miraculous interventions; it was object firing at object, and when that was done, one object would have ceased to operate due to mechanical failure brought about by the penetration of a lead bullet.

At ten, Stanton spun, fired and missed. Quinn saw it. It was deliberate. He stood facing Olive with his chin on his chest, the weapon at his side. Olive held his gun with both hands for steadiness. He had as much time as he wanted and at twenty feet he could explode Stanton's skull in a shower of meat and bone splinter. Quinn saw that Olive's face was swollen with minor injuries but his eyes were open and intent. He raised the end of the gun and fired over Stanton's head. "You bastard!" Stanton roared, as Olive flung the gun into the crowd, running. "Oh, my god, you bastard!" The crowd, now an insane heterogeny of Olive's gang and the club, rushed around Quinn and past him and into the trees, the lights all around him and the sound of voiceless hurrying. Olive was not far in front of them. He was driving himself into a corner where the steep plateau met the river and they were after him, now that Stanton hadn't done his work. Quinn kept up and dodged aside when an old white birch cracked and went down onto the sodden ground. He couldn't see who was leading them and he knew the frontward edge of the horde was well ahead of him. Then they began to pile up in noisy confusion and, deep behind as he was, Quinn realized that they were confronting Earl Olive. Quinn pushed through to where he could see him. He found him, back to the river, transfixed by the beams of all their lights as though he were pierced by them. In his face was a look of transcendent terror and when it was shouted that he was unarmed, they rushed forward. Olive threw himself into the river. The horde rushed down the bank to stay alongside him and kept their lights on his head and the arms that beat the tortuous current around him. Below was a gravel bar and they raced down to it, filing noisily out onto its shallows. Olive floundered helplessly toward them, borne on the fast and gleaming tide. As he neared them, he began to bay that Stanton would make them pay; Stanton wouldn't let anything happen to him, he bayed abjectly. They caught him at the bar and dragged him to land, all falling upon him, grabbing and punching at him. Quinn saw him go under them, only his feet showing, kicking and flailing the air like a baby's. Quinn pushed his way in, found Scott striking at Olive with a heavy root. Quinn kicked Scott mightily in the groin and the crowd took no notice when he fell. One of the mercenaries had Olive by the ears and hair and was trying to drag him to his feet when Quinn nailed him and started beating into the crowd with his fists. They made short work of Quinn, and Scott had the pleasure of tying him up.

A minute later, hands tied in front of him, he was being pushed along beside Olive who was slung from a pole by his ankles and wrists. Olive suffered extremely. They had tied him with a striped silk necktie and Quinn had the impression he would be the centerpiece at a banquet. The blue cowboy shirt had pulled out of the top of his pants to reveal an expanse of flaccid white belly and the whole great torso swung from side to side with the motion of the carriers. Olive's head hung down unexpectedly far as though his neck were too long. He talked brokenly and told Quinn what a letdown this was in his life. He was being treated like a dog. Stanton had treated him like the gent he was by shooting him in a proper duel. Now Quinn knew Stanton had gotten to him. Olive was a believer. He gazed, upside down and ahead, with numb sentimentality and contentment.

They entered the compound, the men and women trudging, the children dancing out ahead with lanterns. They were brought up short. Sitting in the hole where the time capsule had been removed was Stanton. He had set up a tripod-mounted, air-cooled machine gun and he looked set on mayhem. He told them to free Olive, which they did. He and Olive bade goodbye from a distance and Olive leapt crowing into the absolute darkness. As a good measure, they freed Quinn too. Stanton told them to sit down. Anyone who moved, he promised, would be snuffed out. Quinn could see him shaking from here. He was altogether batty now and the machine gun was trained into their midst.

After a couple of hours, they began to fall asleep. Quinn stayed awake for a while thinking that Janey was gone. He could see Stanton, eyes open as though blind, shaking at the grips of the machine gun: the poor man. In a while, Quinn dozed off fitfully. He woke up in the predawn morning and Stanton was still behind the gun like a zombie. He fell asleep again only to wake up a few minutes later to the terrible firing of the gun. Stanton had slumped into the pit and the blazing gun was shuddering with its bursts and explosions of fire. Everyone was bolt upright now as they watched Stanton struggle to train it on them. The belt of ammunition jerked beside the gun and ran into it with terrible slowness. Then Stanton vanished, slumped into the hole again; a long moment later, his hand appeared and hauled on the trigger and the gun raged into the trees over their heads. The belt of ammunition crept, then stopped. There was a long pause; Stanton crawled out of the hole, crazy and confused, and tried to operate the gun. Quinn walked over to him. It was the end.

The police, five of them, came up the main entrance the next day. Quinn, the only member there who saw nothing to hide or preserve, was cooperative. He answered all questions with an agreeable and efficient air. He watched the cops press around the photograph, making a blue shrine of their bodies. He felt this hermetic, outlandish thing punctured at last, a century of bad air expiring. The publicity and uproar that followed that year produced a decline in Quinn's business. The feeling in Detroit was that he had sold his own kind down the river.

Item: The following appeared in *Judson and Judson,* International Real Estate Brokers' annual:

Gentlemen's sporting club with a past! Largest private holding in Northern Michigan! 29,000 acres first and second growth pine and many winding miles of trout teeming Pere Marquette River, both banks! See deer, bear, beavers, birds! Reportedly, small basin could be reestablished by construction of dam! Considerable stockpile of hand-adzed timber and period roofing material! A number of buildings provide convention and conference possibilities. Tempting subdivision potential in this water wonderland northwoods vacation paradise. Region beginning to show promising turnover in A-frame sports-chateau sites and holiday farmettes. Ready access via Highway 76 and nearby airfield which handles up to twin-engined craft. Price and brochure on request. Ask for "Club With A Past," property #1980.

A little thought would have saved the broker's fee. Stanton bought the Centennial Club the day it was offered.

He generously deeded Quinn's house to him. They met the following January. Stanton fetched him at the front gate in the cutter between whose restored shafts was a beautiful Morgan gelding, fat as a pullet, and flecked with dark gray in its lighter gray coat. Stanton introduced the stableboy, a cultivated young man in an Icelandic sweater who said he would walk back. Stanton was thinner and Quinn wondered if he himself could have aged so. They rode silently under blankets as the horse picked its way down the path off the plateau and came beneath the ridge that was now a white bluff of snow onto the lake bed. Quinn stole a look at Stanton whose features had clarified impressively under madness and loss of weight. He seemed heroic and at one with his illusions. Stanton threw ripples down the reins and the gelding picked up its stride until the runners hissed and the wind lifted the long winter mane of the horse. Quinn watched him smile up into a sky of no stars whatsoever with a bearing of unspecific mastery. Quinn's face tightened pleasantly under the cold sting of wind. Stark ridges of pine enclosed their circle of snow. "James, old pal," Stanton said, "you have outlasted me. Learned persons have expressed doubt that I am ever coming back . . ." His voice trailed away content.

When they got to the house, the stableboy was somehow waiting for them again with the butler, another keen young man with a clipboard and indeterminate crewcut. This one took their coats impatiently. They passed into the house, the young men sticking close to their elbows. Stanton stopped suddenly in the hallway and said to the two, "Stand back, you bastards, now. I need room to breathe." They fell away a bit. Stanton started upstairs to change for dinner and the two, hovering under the moose head, watched him ascend. He caught Quinn's eye with a smile and turned to them again. "Just because none of you can hit the bowl," he pronounced, "you think everyone should walk barefoot in your pee. I don't buy it." He continued up the stairs and the two fluttered into his wake. When they were close, he turned and feinted at them; they fell back and Stanton went up laughing.

Waiting for dinner, Quinn and Janey talked to each other with careful familial heartiness. She had pictures of a visit Stanton had made to Texas the previous year. One showed him standing in front of a parked car with a cloud of alkali dust still hanging in the air behind. The photograph caught him with a wide, blind smile on his face and a wax-paper cone of roses in his hand. The car nudges an adobe barbecue in the sun, miles from the champagne cellars of Waco. Another shows him with Mom and Dad in the hot fog of the mineral spring. They all three wave as if showing written messages on the palms of their hands.

At dinner they had platters of partridge and wild rice, two bottles of cold Traminer. Stanton talked well when he remembered; he never faltered from forgetting but stopped cleanly and waited for Janey to cue him. Afterward, they went downstairs to the gallery. Stanton no longer had his pistols; but he had plywood cutouts that were much the same; and they paced off, turned and said "Bang, bang!" at each other soberly. Then someone invisible upstairs announced Stanton's bedtime. Quinn went up then too; though it wasn't until later, in bed and still awake in the big, strangely stilled house, that he felt each of their presences, compromised and happy, each asleep and dreaming, like bees in cells of honey.